T0018084

PENGUIN MODERN CLASSICS

Four Chapters

RABINDRANATH TAGORE (1861–1941) was one of the key figures of the Bengal Renaissance. He started writing at an early age, and by the turn of the century, he had become a household name in Bengal as a poet, a songwriter, a playwright, an essayist, a short story writer and a novelist. In 1913, he was awarded the Nobel Prize for Literature for his verse collection *Gitanjali*. Around the same time, he founded Visva Bharati, a university located in Santiniketan, near Kolkata. Called the 'Great Sentinel' of modern India by Mahatma Gandhi, Tagore steered clear of active politics but is famous for returning the knighthood conferred on him as a gesture of protest against the Jallianwala Bagh massacre in 1919.

Tagore was a pioneering literary figure, renowned for his ceaseless innovations in poetry, prose, drama, music and painting, which he took up late in life. His works include some sixty collections of verse, novels like *Gora*, *Chokher Bali* and *Ghare Baire*, plays like *Raktakarabi* and *Dakghar*, dance dramas like *Shyama*, *Chandalika* and *Chitrangada*, over a hundred short stories, essays on religious, social and literary topics, and over 2500 songs, including the national anthems of India and Bangladesh.

RADHA CHAKRAVARTY is a writer, critic and translator. She has co-edited *The Essential Tagore*, nominated Book of the Year 2011 by Martha Nussbaum. She is the author of *Feminism and Contemporary Women Writers* and *Novelist Tagore: Gender and Modernity in Selected Texts*. Her Tagore translations include *Gora*, *Chokher Bali*, *Boyhood Days*, *Farewell Song: Shesher Kabita* and *The Land of Cards: Stories, Poems and Plays for Children*. Other works in translation are Bankimchandra Chatterjee's *Kapalkundala*, Mahasweta Devi's *Our Santiniketan* and *In the Name of the Mother* (nominated for the Crossword Translation Award, 2004), *Vermillion Clouds: Stories by Bengali Women*, and *Crossings: Stories from Bangladesh and India*. She has edited *Shades of Difference: Selected Writings of Rabindranath*

Tagore and *Bodymaps: Stories by South Asian Women*, and co-edited *Writing Feminism: South Asian Voices* and *Writing Freedom: South Asian Voices*. Her poems have appeared in numerous anthologies and journals. She has contributed to *Pandemic: A Worldwide Community Poem* (Muse Pie Press, USA), nominated for the Pushcart Prize 2020. Forthcoming books include *The Tagore Phenomenon*, *Mahasweta Devi: Writer, Activist, Visionary*, and Kazi Nazrul Islam's essays in translation. Radha Chakravarty is Professor of Comparative Literature & Translation Studies at Dr. B. R. Ambedkar University Delhi.

RABINDRANATH TAGORE

Four Chapters

Translated from the Bengali by Radha Chakravarty

PENGUIN BOOKS

An imprint of Penguin Random House

PENGUIN BOOKS

USA | Canada | UK | Ireland | Australia
New Zealand | India | South Africa | China

Penguin Books is part of the Penguin Random House group of companies
whose addresses can be found at global.penguinrandomhouse.com

Published by Penguin Random House India Pvt. Ltd
4th Floor, Capital Tower 1, MG Road,
Gurugram 122 002, Haryana, India

Penguin
Random House
India

First published in English in Penguin Books by Penguin Random House India 2022

English translation and introduction copyright © Radha Chakravarty 2022

All rights reserved

10 9 8 7 6 5 4 3 2 1

This is a work of fiction. Names, characters, places and incidents are either the
product of the author's imagination or are used fictitiously, and any resemblance
to any actual person, living or dead, events or locales is entirely coincidental.

ISBN 9780143452645

Typeset in Bembo Std by Manipal Technologies Limited, Manipal
Printed at Replika Press Pvt. Ltd, India

This book is sold subject to the condition that it shall not, by way of trade
or otherwise, be lent, resold, hired out, or otherwise circulated without the
publisher's prior consent in any form of binding or cover other than that in
which it is published and without a similar condition including this condition
being imposed on the subsequent purchaser.

www.penguin.co.in

MIX
Paper from
responsible sources
FSC® C016779

Translator's Dedication

To Abhishek Chakravarty and Radha Kapuria

Contents

Introduction

Radha Chakravarty

Rabindranath Tagore's controversial last novel *Char Adhyay* (Four Chapters) appeared in 1341 BE (December 1934) as a complete book. Unlike his other novels, it was not serialized before its publication as a book. At the heart of the narrative lies the internal conflict of the female protagonist Ela, a free-spirited young woman who has been brought up in her uncle's household after being orphaned very young. Educated and high-spirited, Ela feels stifled by her aunt's petty jealousy and turns against the idea of marriage. She succumbs instead to the charisma of Indranath, a scientific man and political activist who espouses the path of terror in the name of nationalism. She joins his cause, taking the vow never to marry, and takes up the position of headmistress of a school, as a cover for her underground nationalist activities. In spite of her vow, she becomes romantically involved with the poet and romantic Atindra, who, despite his aristocratic birth, gets involved in the political struggle and falls in love with her. Although Ela and Atin acknowledge their mutual attraction, they are prevented from marrying because of the vow that Ela has taken. Eventually, Ela becomes disenchanted with Indranath's false political claims and ruthless, manipulative politics. Because she knows too much, her alienation makes her a threat to the group. The novel charts the volatile scenario that arises from the conflict between Ela's forbidden love and her dangerous involvement with political violence. Through the relationships between Ela, Atin and Indranath, the narrative explores the interface between love and revolutionary politics.

In the first draft of the novel, Tagore placed the romantic plot centre stage. As for the theme of nationalism, Ela was represented as Gandhi's follower and a promoter of khaddar. The text had three chapters, and the character of Indranath did not figure in it. The final version, comprising the four chapters that give the novel its title, introduces Indranath as a lead actor in the drama and derives its tension and vibrancy from the inclusion of the political plot and its integral connection with the love story.

In his portrayal of Indranath, it is probable that Tagore had in mind the figure of Brahmabandhab Upadhyay (1861–1907), activist, editor and scholar of Vendanta philosophy and Catholic theology, who championed the idea of using terror as a political instrument. The first edition of *Char Adhyay* included an 'Abhash' (Pre-text), where Tagore describes Upadhyay's magnetic influence. He also recounts their final meeting, when, at the moment of departure, Upadhyay suddenly turns round at the threshold and says: 'Robibabu, I have greatly fallen' (Tagore 2002: 138). Tagore observes though that the man was so deeply embroiled in his predicament that there was no possibility of release for him. The 'Abhash' was dropped from the second edition of *Char Adhyay*, which appeared six months after, in 1342 BE (*c.*1935). Historical events such as the Chittagong Armoury Raid (24 September 1932) and the nationalist assault on Sir John Anderson, Lieutenant Governor of Bengal (10 May 1934), may have also provided real-life inspiration for Tagore's novel. Upon finishing the final draft of his novel, Tagore wrote a letter to Prafullanath Tagore (8 August 1934), saying: 'You are aware that I am completely against the oppressive tactics of those who follow the path of terrorism . . . I have written a work of fiction that is cast as a protest against the terrorists'.[1]

Tagore's critique of the use of terror and coercion in revolutionary politics aroused the wrath of many compatriots who accused him of being disloyal to the nation. His challenge to authoritarianism and insistence on freedom of thought also invoked the displeasure and suspicion of the British administration in India. Although he knew that his novel had such inflammatory content, Tagore was not deterred from publishing it. Anticipating that his book might be banned by the British, he urged Amiya Chakravarty to translate it into English, so that it could reach audiences outside India. In fact, even after

printing, the book's publication was withheld for several
months, until December 1934 (Mukhopadhyay 1952: 383).

Predictably, a furore broke out upon the appearance of
Char Adhyay. Bengali nationalists serving prison sentences
in different parts of the country reacted with outrage and
disbelief against what they considered a one-sided narrative
that failed to represent their cause. 'Why did Rabindranath—
our Rabindranath—write this book? Why did he write it
at this precise moment when the whole of Bengal is in the
grip of the Andersonian dance of destruction?' wrote Saroj
Acharya in his memoirs, voicing the sentiment of many of
his compatriots.[2] Admirers of Brahmabandhab Upadhyay
also protested intensely against the 'Abhash',[3] forcing
Tagore to withdraw the piece from the second edition of
his novel.

Tagore countered his critics in a 'Kaifiyat' (Response),
which appeared in the periodical *Prabasi* in 1935, asserting
that his novel is primarily a love story: 'The only thing that
may properly be called the theme of this narrative is the love
between Ela and Atindra' (Tagore 2002: 143). He insisted:
'the specific dramatic dimension of this love has found a
resonance in the context of the revolutionary movement
in Bengal. In this text, the description of this revolution is
secondary' (Tagore 2002: 146-7). Yet, no reader of *Char
Adhyay* can fail to notice that the love story and the narrative
of a revolution gone awry are inseparably woven together.

In fact, Tagore's views on nationalism had always been
controversial. In novels such as *Gora* and *Ghare Baire* and
the lectures collected in *Nationalism*, he had expressed

complex ideas on different versions of nationalism, risking the ire of audiences in India and abroad. After his initial participation in the Swadeshi movement in the early twentieth century, he had grown disillusioned with the violent and communal elements that became evident in some strands of the movement. Withdrawing from direct involvement in the movement, he had taken to fiction as a creative way to express his thoughts on nationalism. In *Char Adhyay* as well, we find a new and different phase in the evolution of Tagore's ideas on nation, revolution and human freedom. 'If *Ghare-Baire* reflects Tagore's impression of the public face of revolutionary politics, *Char Adhyay* seeks to expose its private face and the dehumanization that goes with it' (Ramkrishna Bhattacharya 2006: 141). Here, through the character of Ela, the woman's psyche emerges as the site where ideological conflicts can be staged and also the place from where resistance and transformation can be reimagined.[4]

In the 1930s, while Gandhi led the Salt Satyagraha, militant nationalism was also emerging as a powerful force, and women were joining both modes of resistance (Ray 2004: 15). Under the leadership of Aurobindo's niece Latika Ghosh, during the Calcutta Congress of 1928, 100 women had volunteered for such political work. The women scholars of Bethune College maintained regular contact with the revolutionary groups. In Tagore's novel, Ela's story depicts the ways in which women's emergence in the public sphere impacted their lives. She is more highly educated than some of Tagore's other heroines and also very independent and

free-spirited. She rejects arranged marriage and opts instead
to take up a career and join the political movement. She
can engage in intellectual arguments with Indranath and
ultimately distances herself from his cold-blooded, cynical
philosophy of life. Yet, the text also indicates how the
figure of the woman is objectified and exploited within the
domain of nationalist politics. Indranath seeks to deify Ela,
placing her on a pedestal to influence the masses. Botu, on
the other hand, wants to degrade her to the status of a sexual
victim. In their different ways, both seek to use Ela as an
object, without acknowledging her individuality.

Ela's relationship with Atin helps her to resist such
forms of enslavement. Her political awakening becomes
transformed into a sexual awakening through her encounter
with Atin. Her search for sexual freedom, articulated
eloquently in her plea for a Gandharva marriage, expresses
her questioning of societal norms. Significantly, this
assertive image of the woman as a desiring subject derives
from indigenous tradition and not from a Western model
of women's sexual liberation. Herein lies a clue to Tagore's
search for a textual modernity that resembles yet does not
imitate emerging forms of modernity in the West.

Tagore's last novel interrogates conventional
constructions of masculinity and femininity. For instance,
stereotypical notions of masculinity are challenged through
Ela's repudiation of Indranath's will to power. She also
questions Indranath's bid to control her sexuality through the
imposition of the pledge of celibacy. The relationship of Ela
and Atin counters the cold-blooded, scientific mechanics of

control that express Indranath's will to dominate. It is Atin who impels Ela to recognize that she has been ensnared, her freedom circumscribed, by Indranath's attempt to cast her in an idealized role. In place of Indranath's heartless rationality, their mutual love is premised on qualities of what Dipesh Chakravarty (2000: 51) refers to as 'hriday' or the heart, offering a paradigm for an alternative modern subjectivity that does not derive from the Western ideal of reason.

All the same, even while Ela stakes her claim to freedom and agency in their mutual relationship, she continues to adopt a subservient position vis-à-vis Atin, referring to herself as his 'sevika' or handmaiden. The text also signals that Atin does not really accept complete parity between man and woman. Although he critiques Indranath's authoritarianism, he also tries to convince Ela that her true womanliness lies in her skills at nurture and domesticity (M. Bhattacharya 1995: 235). Throughout their final dialogues, Ela asserts her love for Atin as an affirmation of her freedom, but Atin tries to fight his passion for her, insisting that he must rise above his sexual desire to strive towards a more exalted goal. Ela's quest for freedom remains caught in her own inner contradictions as well as Atin's refusal to succumb. The novel suggests that despite their bold self-assertions, neither of them is fully ready to accept such a radical transformation of gendered power relations in society. The text does not offer neat solutions to these issues. Amartya Sen regards this refusal of oversimplification, this 'celebration of the unresolved and the incomplete' as a remarkable element in

Tagore's writing, signalling his humility in the face of a vast universe that escapes our full comprehension (Sen 2007: xx).

Like Tagore's dance dramas *Chitrangada* and *Shyama* and his novels *Chokher Bali* and *Chaturanga*, *Char Adhyay* is modern in the way it tackles the theme of female physical desire boldly and directly. When Ela enters the dark, menacing jungle to meet Atin in the ruined house, the language invokes a scene that is simultaneously exterior and interior, both real and psychological, a place that is also no-place (asthaan in the Bengali), an inversion of the lovers' tryst, a journey leading not to union but annihilation. Ela's real encounter is not with Atin but with the inner psychological landscape of her own sexuality and hidden desires. The ruined house also represents the remnants of history, the vestiges of the past that Ela seeks to challenge with her new, yet age-old defiance of social convention.

Char Adhyay is also experimental in its approach to style and form. It is as if Tagore was looking for a new literary aesthetic that would suit the altered reality of a world in transition. The structure of the book, comprising the Prelude and four chapters, presents a deliberately fractured shape, emphasizing gaps in time and dislocations in space that separate the different segments of the narrative. Rimli Bhattacharya argues that '*Char Adhyay*'s complete break with linearity at a fundamental level is integral to Rabindranath's discourse on modern subjectivity' (2002: 111). In this novel, dialogue predominates over narrative and action. Tagore seems to be breaking the boundaries that separate different genres. Buddhadeva Basu argues that the four chapters can be reimagined as four acts of a play and also that despite its affinity to dramatic form, the text actually is lyrical in spirit (1983: 114–116). At this stage in his life, Tagore was also intensely involved in painting. Some of the settings described in *Char Adhyay* have a vivid pictorial quality, as if he was not only crossing generic boundaries but also the lines that divide one creative medium from another. This transcendence of generic limits sets Tagore's novel apart from the modern novel in the West, demanding a reconsideration of the possibilities inherent in the novel form itself.

Some readers fault the novel for political and historical inaccuracies. It has been pointed out, for example, that the image of Ela presents a confusing mix of two different forms of nationalism, combining the Gandhian support for Khaddar with the espousal of secret societies advocating extremism (Ramkrishna Bhattacharya 2006: 142). It may be argued that this does not flag Tagore's lack of political awareness but expresses, rather, his creative license in using fiction to explore and articulate his own outlook on history and politics. Like Saratchandra Chatterjee and Tarasankar Bandyopadhyay, Tagore too can be regarded as one of the early practitioners of the Bengali novel about politics.

Char Adhyay is not an easy text to translate. Although Tagore exhorted Amiya Chakravarty to translate the novel into English even while the Bengali book was still in the pipeline, he was very critical of the translation when Chakravarty shared it with him. The translation never saw the light of day. In 1950, Visva-Bharati published

Surendranath Tagore's English translation. A modern, evocative translation by Rimli Bhattacharya appeared in 2002. Film adaptations of the novel include the Hindi version directed by Kumar Shahani in 1997 and the Bengali adaptations 'Elar Char Adhyay' by Bappaditya Bandyopadhyay (2012) and 'Char Adhyay' by Nitish Mukherjee (2016). The present translation attempts to bring the text closer to the contemporary reader, even while evoking the atmosphere of a historical moment from the past. This has proved a difficult challenge, as also the choices faced by the translator when dealing with concepts and ideas that are culture-specific. Many indigenous words have been retained to sustain the localized flavour of the text. There has been little attempt to smoothen Tagore's language as that might compromise the dramatic immediacy of the language of this extraordinary, dialogue-rich novel.

Char Adhyay retains its power to unsettle readers even now, almost a century after it first appeared. The contemporary reader who listens closely to Tagore's text can experience the intensity and urgency with which it still speaks to us in today's world, across the distances imposed by time, geography and language.

References

Basu, Buddhadeva. 1983. *Rabindranath: Kathasahitya* (Bengali), 1955. Kolkata: New Age.

Bhattacharya, Anuttam. 2008. *Rabindra Rachanabhidhan* (Bengali) Vol. 8. Kolkata: Deep Prakashan.

Bhattacharya, Malini. 1995. 'Rabindrachintaye o Srishtite Narimuktir Bhavana' (Bengali), in *Nirmaner Samajikata o Adunik Bangla Upanyas*, 84–98. Kolkata: Dey's.

Bhattacharya, Ramkrishna. 2006. 'Rabindranath Tagore and the Politicization of the Bangla novel', in Krishna Sen and Tapati Gupta (eds.), *Tagore and Modernity*, 136–148. Kolkata: Dasgupta and Co.

Bhattacharya, Rimli. 2002. 'On translating *Char Adhyay*', in Rabindranath Tagore, *Four Chapters*, 109–134.

Chakrabarty, Dipesh. 2000. 'Witness to Suffering: Domestic Cruelty and the Birth of the Modern Subject in Bengal', in Timothy Mitchell (ed.), *Questions of Modernity*, Minneapolis: University of Minnesota Press. 49–86.

Chakravarty, Radha. 2013. *Novelist Tagore: Gender and Modernity in Selected Texts*. London and New Delhi: Routledge.

Kar, Sisir. 1990. *British Shasane Bajeyapta Bangla Boi* (Bengali). Kolkata: Ananda Publishers.

Mukhopadhyay, Prabhatkumar. 1952. *Rabindra Jibani* Vol. 3 (Bengali). Kolkata: Visva-Bharati.

Ray, Mohit Kumar. 2004. *Studies on Rabindranath Tagore*, Vol. 1. New Delhi: Atlantic Publishers.

Sen, Amartya. 2007. 'Introduction', in Rabindranath Tagore, *Boyhood Days*, trans. Radha Chakravarty, pp. ix–xxiii. New Delhi: Penguin India/Puffin Classics.

Tagore, Rabindranath. 2002. *Four Chapters* (*Char Adhyay*), trans. Rimli Bhattacharya. New Delhi: Srishti.

Notes

1. Tagore's letter was published in *Dainik Basumati* (Autumn 1969), 14. See A. Bhattacharya 2008: 411.

2. Saroj Acharya, *Rachanabali* vol. 2 (Bengali), 286-7, cited in A. Bhattacharya 2008: 412.

3. See Bhupendranath Datta, "Bhumika" (Preface) to Balai Debsarmma, *Brahmabandhab Upadhyay* (Kolkata: Prabrattak Publishers, 1961), iv, xiii, cited in Ramkrishna Bhattacharya 146. See also Sisir Kar 114-125.

4. For a detailed analysis of these aspects of the text, see Chakravarty 2013.

Four Chapters

Prelude

Ela remembered that her life first announced its existence through rebellion. Her mother, Mayamoyi, was driven by idiosyncratic compulsions, unable to adhere to the wide avenues of reason and reflection. Propelled by the uncontrolled stormy gusts of her whimsical temperament, she raised hell in the household at random times, inflicted unjust punishments, and suspected people without reason. 'You're lying!', Mayamoyi would insist when her daughter denied such accusations. However, the girl had a habit of telling the unadulterated truth; in fact, it was virtually an addiction. As a consequence, she bore the brunt of all the punishment. Her nature had developed a pronounced intolerance against all sorts of injustice. To her mother, this seemed contrary to the dharma prescribed for women.

One thing that Ela had recognized since her childhood was that weakness is the prime vehicle for oppression. The very people who depended on her family for shelter and livelihood, helplessly bound by the largesse or chastisement meted out by others, had poisoned the atmosphere of their domestic life and allowed her mother's blind authoritarianism to flourish unchecked. It was as a reaction to this unhealthy environment that, from a young age, Ela's desire for independence had grown so irrepressible.

Ela's father, Naresh Dasgupta, had returned from an English university with a degree in psychology. Gifted with scientific acumen, he became a distinguished academic and teacher. He had accepted a position in a regional private college because he was born in that place and possessed little greed and negligible aptitude for worldly advancement. A series of recurring experiences had not amended his tendency to bring harm upon himself by placing mistaken trust in people. The ingratitude of those who manage to obtain benefits by guile or without effort is the most heartless of all. When such instances came to light, however, he would simply acknowledge such behaviour as a special psychological trait without any verbal or mental rancour. For the many flaws in his financial judgement, he had never received his wife's forgiveness and had to face her remonstrations every day. Even past grievances would not be forgotten. Randomly, at will, his wife would fan the flames, refusing to let the fire subside. Watching her father being repeatedly cheated or harmed due to his large, trusting heart, Ela felt a constant, painful affection for him—the kind of tender love a mother feels towards her infant son. What pained her the most was when her mother's rants pointedly insinuated that in matters of judgement, she was her husband's superior. On many occasions, Ela had witnessed her father's humiliation at her mother's hands. At night, her tears of helpless resentment would wet the pillow. Often, Ela could not help but blame her father because such excessive patience on his part was a mistake in her eyes.

'It's wrong to put up with such wrongs in silence,' she had once protested to him in extreme agitation.

'To oppose someone's innate nature is like stroking red-hot iron with one's palm in an attempt to cool it down,' Naresh had responded. 'That may be brave, but it brings no comfort.'

'Enduring things silently brings even less comfort,' Ela retorted and stormed out of the scene.

Meanwhile, within the household, Ela could see that the intrigues of those wily enough to appease her mother were leading to the perpetration of brutal injustice upon the guiltless. Unable to bear this, Ela in her agitation tried to present evidence of the truth before the woman who presided as judge. But to the ego of the arbitrating authority, irrefutable facts appeared like signs of insufferable impertinence. Instead of propelling the boat of reason forward like a propitious gusty breeze, such arguments made it keel over.

Within this household, another practice which offended Ela's sensibilities on a daily basis was her mother's fetish for ritual cleanliness and purity. Once, Ela had spread out a madur on the floor to welcome a Muslim visitor. Her mother threw out the straw mat. Offering a galchey—a woven carpet—would have been acceptable. With her bent for rational analysis, Ela could not resist an argument.

'Why is it that women in particular are obsessed with all this fuss about purity and touch, all these strict rituals of bathing and eating without contamination?' an indignant Ela had once asked her father. 'The heart has no place in all this. Rather, it smacks of a negative attitude, contrary to the truth of things. Indeed, it amounts to blindly following rules, just like a machine.'

'Women's minds have been shackled for a thousand years,' her psychologist father had replied. 'Their lot is to obey, not to ask questions. This attitude has been rewarded by the social system and by their masters. The more blindly women follow norms, the more they stand to gain. This is also the plight of men who appear effeminate.'

Ela could not resist the urge to constantly challenge her mother about the meaninglessness of these codes of purity. She was also repeatedly answered with admonitions. On account of these daily confrontations, Ela's mind had grown inclined towards disobedience.

Realizing that these family duels were affecting his daughter's health, Naresh felt intensely anxious. Meanwhile, deeply wounded by a particular instance of injustice, Ela came to her father one day.

'Baba, send me to a boarding house in Kolkata,' she demanded.

A painful proposal for both of them, but Naresh understood the situation and, despite a storm of opposition from Mayamoyi, he sent Ela away to a distant place. Amidst the bitter atmosphere of his own household, he immersed himself in study and teaching.

'If you wish to turn your daughter into a memsahib by sending her off to the city, then go ahead,' warned Mayamoyi. 'But that spoilt daughter of yours will have to suffer untold misery once she moves to her marital home. When that happens, don't blame me.'

Discerning in her daughter's conduct the evil signs of an independence fit for Kalikal—the fatally sinful, apocalyptic age of modernity—Mayamoyi voiced these fears on many occasions. She was vocal in expressing her sympathy for Ela's future mother-in-law, convinced that her daughter would very likely drive that imaginary housewife out of her wits. This in turn had led Ela to believe that to prepare themselves for marriage, girls were required to paralyze their self-respect and numb their sense of justice.

When Ela entered college after her matriculation, her mother passed away. Naresh sometimes tried to get his daughter to consent to the occasional proposal of marriage. Ela was exquisitely beautiful and had no lack of suitors, but she was averse to marriage by virtue of her convictions. Soon after she cleared her examinations, her father died, leaving his daughter unmarried.

Suresh was his youngest brother. Naresh had raised him and funded his education throughout. For supporting his brother's studies in England, Naresh had been taunted by his wife and hounded by moneylenders. Suresh was now a high-ranking employee of the postal department. His work took him to various regions. It was upon him that

the responsibility of looking after Ela had fallen after his
brother's death. He accepted the burden with a great deal
of care and concern.

Suresh's wife Madhavi came from a family where it was
customary for women to have limited education. Indeed,
their level of learning was below average. When Suresh
travelled to far-off places after his return from England,
he had to socialize with all sorts of people from the wider
world. After a while, Madhavi had grown habituated to
following foreign customs in her social interactions. In fact,
even in white people's clubs, she could get by with her
halting English, covering her lapses with warranted and
unwarranted laughter.

When Ela entered their household, Suresh was posted
in a big city. With her beauty, talents and education, she
evoked her kaka's pride. He grew eager to present Ela to
his superiors and colleagues as well as his Indian and English
acquaintances on some pretext or the other. It did not take
long for Ela's feminine instinct to warn her that this would
affect her adversely. Feigning relief, Madhavi had taken to
repeatedly saying, 'What a blessing! Why burden me with
the task of socializing in the English style, bapu? I have
neither education, nor beauty.'

Observing her attitude, Ela created a wall around herself
as if locking herself into a zenana, the private women's
quarters in a house. With excessive zeal, she took up the
duty of tutoring Suresh's daughter Surama. She devoted the
remainder of her time to writing a thesis on a comparative
study of Bengali Mangalkavyas and the poetry of Chaucer.

Suresh was very excited about this project. He boasted to all and sundry about it.

'A bit much!' commented Madhavi, pulling a face.

'You suddenly placed your daughter under Ela's tutelage,' she protested to her husband. 'Why, what wrong has the tutor Adhar Master committed? Say what you will, but I must point out . . .'

'What's this!' exclaimed Suresh, in surprise. 'To compare Ela with Adhar!'

'Merely memorizing the contents of a couple of notebooks to pass examinations doesn't make one educated,' Madhavi retorted. With these words, the mistress of the house stormed out of the room.

There was something she hesitated to articulate, even to her husband. Madhavi mused to herself, 'Surama will soon pass the age of thirteen. Before we know it, we will have to comb the region in search of a suitor. For Ela to be around at such a time, given these young men's fetish for a fair complexion . . . What do they know about true beauty, anyway?' Sighing, she reflected that it was futile to say such things to her husband. Men were blind to worldly things, after all.

The lady of the house now made it her urgent business to get Ela married off as fast as possible. It did not take much effort. Desirable suitors appeared on their own—suitors whom Madhavi began to covet for her own Surama. But Ela would turn them away, dashing their hopes time and again.

Suresh grew anxious at his bhaijhi's obstinate lack of judgement. Ela's kaki became extremely impatient and intolerant, aware that it was regarded as almost criminal for a Bengali girl who had come of age to slight a good suitor. She began to fear all sorts of mishaps that might befall a girl of Ela's age, and her heart was overcome with a heavy sense of responsibility. It became clear to Ela that she was poised to trigger a conflict between her kaka's affection for her and the atmosphere in his household.

At this juncture, Indranath arrived in the city. The students in the area revered him like a ruling monarch. His energy was extraordinary, as was his reputation as a scholar. One day, he was invited to Suresh's house. Although they had not been introduced to each other, Ela came up to him and asked without coyness:

'Can't you involve me in some of your work?'

Such a request was not particularly surprising in those times, but Indranath was struck by the girl's radiant spirit.

'Narayani High School for girls has been recently established in Kolkata,' he responded. 'I can offer you the position of headmistress. Are you ready to accept it?'

'I am ready, if you are willing to trust me.'

'I am a good judge of character,' Indranath declared, fixing her with his shining gaze. 'It didn't take me even a second to place my trust in you. At the very first sight, I recognized you as the harbinger of a new age. You carry within you the call of a new era.'

Hearing these words on Indranath's lips, Ela felt a sudden tremor in her heart.

'Your words strike me with awe,' she replied. 'Please don't form a false, exaggerated impression of me. If I try in vain to live up to that impression, it will break me. I will try to keep your ideals alive to the best of my limited ability, but I won't be able to keep up a pretence.'

'You will have to take a vow to never let yourself be confined by domestic ties,' Indranath pronounced. 'You do not belong to society. You belong to the nation.'

'That is my vow,' Ela declared, raising her head.

When Ela was about to depart, her kaka urged:

'I will never again speak to you of marriage. Remain here with me. Why don't you start a small class here to teach the girls of the neighbourhood?'

'She's old enough,' argued Madhavi, irked by her doting husband's lack of wisdom. 'If she wants to take charge of her own life, that's just as well. Why try to stop her? I don't care what you might think, but I can't take on the burden of worrying for her, let me tell you.'

'I have found employment,' Ela insisted with great vehemence. 'I will go and assume my duties.'

Thus, Ela departed to assume her duties as headmistress.

Five years have passed since this prelude. The story has now advanced much further.

1

The scene: a tea shop. Adjoining it is a small room where some school and college textbooks, many of them second-hand, are displayed for sale. Some of them are English translations of modern European stories and plays. Boys, often out of money, come in, browse and leave. The proprietor of the shop, Kanai Gupta, does not object. He is a pensioner, a former sub-inspector in the police force.

The shop faces the main road and is flanked by an alley on the left. For those who wish to enjoy their tea in seclusion, part of the room has been screened off with tattered sacking. Today, in that partitioned area, signs of some special arrangements can be seen. To compensate for the shortage of stools and chairs, some packing cases bearing the stamp of a Darjeeling tea company have been placed there. Even the pieces of crockery have clashing designs. Some cups are made of blue enamel, others are of white china. On the table, a bunch of flowers, arranged in a milk jug with a broken handle.

It was almost three in the afternoon. When they invited Elalata, the boys had insisted that two-thirty was the precise time for the appointment. Even a minute's delay wouldn't do. An odd time for an invitation, but that was when the shop would be empty. From four-thirty onwards, a crowd would assemble there, thirsting for tea.

Ela arrived punctually. But there was no sign of the boys—not a single one. She waited alone, wondering if she had made a mistake about the date. Presently, Indranath entered the room. She started, for there was no likelihood of encountering him in such a place.

Indranath had spent a long time in Europe. He had earned great renown within the scientific field. He was entitled to a high position in his own land as he had glowing letters of reference from European professors. While in Europe, he had occasionally met Indians blacklisted for political reasons. Upon returning to his home country, it was this shameful fact that proved to be a stumbling block for all his endeavours. Eventually, on the strength of a special recommendation from a famous English scientist, he obtained a position as professor, but, this placed him under the authority of an unworthy superior. Unworthiness is usually accompanied by excessive jealousy. Indranath's attempts at scientific research began to be sabotaged by his boss at every stage. Finally, he was transferred to a place that did not have a laboratory. Indranath came to realize that in this land, the path to pursuing his highest aspirations was closed. He could not bear to face the dreadful prospect of a future where he would spend his last days on a meagre pension after the endless grind of the teaching routine. He knew for sure that he had the calibre, in abundant measure, to gain renown in any other country of the world.

Eventually, Indranath started a private coaching centre for lessons in German and French. Alongside, he also took to tutoring college students in botany and geology. Gradually, from the hidden depths of this institution, a secret cause took seed and spread its roots across prison courtyards, creating a vast, complex network.

'Ela, what brings you here?' Indranath enquired.

'You forbade the boys to visit me at home,' Ela responded. 'That is why they have called me to this place.'

'I received news of that earlier and immediately dispatched them elsewhere on urgent work. I have come to apologize on their behalf. I will repay the bill as well.'

'Why did you ruin my party?'

'To suppress the fact that you empathize with the boys. Tomorrow, you will find an article in your name which I have sent off to the papers.'

'Did you write the article? Pseudonyms don't suit your pen. People won't believe that it is not forged.'

'It is unformed writing, left-handed. No sign of intelligence, just some good advice.'

'What does that mean?'

'You write that the boys are set to destroy the country through untimely action. To the women of Bengal, you make an emotional appeal—they should try to pacify the rage of these wretched boys. You say that scolding from afar will not reach their ears; it will be essential to plunge into their midst, to get to the heart of their collective intoxication. The authorities may indeed grow suspicious. So be it. You say: "O race of mothers, if you can save the boys even by taking their punishment upon your own heads, your deaths will be worthwhile." You reiterate the phrase "O race of mothers!" I have set those words, soaked in salt tears, in the very heart of your written piece. Those words will bring tears to the eyes of maternal readers. Had you been a man, it would not have been impossible for you to win the title of Raibahadur after such a stellar performance.'

'I can't say that the words you have written are utterly impossible to pass off as my own. I love these suicidal boys. Where can you find boys like them? They were my collegemates once! At first, they wrote all sorts of nonsense about me on the blackboard. They'd call out from the back of the classroom, addressing me as Chhoto Elaach—small green cardamom—and instantly look away at the sky, feigning innocence! My friend Indrani was a fourth-year student. They called her Boro Elaach—big black cardamom. The poor girl—she was wide of girth and her complexion wasn't dazzling either. Many girls would object to such minor taunts, but I took the side of the boys. I knew it was because they were unaccustomed to the sight of us girls that they lost their balance and sometimes even made offensive remarks. But that was not intrinsic to their nature. When they got accustomed to our presence, they were able to interact with us more easily. Chhoto Elaach became Ela di. Occasionally, some of their voices acquired a hint of honey —and why not? It never made me afraid. From experience,

I have learned that it is very easy to deal with boys, as long as girls don't consciously or unconsciously try to hunt them down. After that phase, I found that one by one, the best of the boys—those who were not narrow-minded, who respected women as worthy men should . . .'

'In other words, those who don't let their desires ferment and froth over, unlike the smart young men of Kolkata . . .'

'Yes, they are the ones I am talking about. The ones in desperate pursuit of death's messenger. Most of them are Bangals, hailing from East Bengal like me. If they run after death, I don't want to remain alive, safe in my domestic corner. But look, Mastermoshai, let me tell you the truth. With the passage of time, my purpose is growing into an addiction rather than an objective. Our efforts seem to proceed at a random pace, guided by our whims, without rhythm, beyond the limits of reason. I don't like this. All those boys seem to be surrendered up for sacrifice at the altar of some blind power. It makes my heart burst.'

'My child, this very repugnance is the prologue to the epic battle of Kurukshetra. Arjun too had been overcome with repulsion. When I started studying medicine, I had almost fainted in disgust at the prospect of dissecting a corpse. That disgust is itself disgusting. At the root of power lies the pursuit of cruelty; forgiveness perhaps comes at the end. You say—all of you—that women are a race of mothers. But that is not something to glory in. After all, mothers are created by nature in the natural course of things. Even animals are no exception. What matters more is that women embody Shakti—power personified. That is what you must prove, moving beyond the swamps of kindness and tenderness to set foot on firmer ground. Power! Give men power!'

'You are trying to distract us with all these grand pronouncements. You project us in an exaggerated light. We cannot live up to such extreme demands!'

'Demands are realized only by the strength of what they assert. Whatever we believe you women to be, that is what you will become. Likewise, you, too, must believe in us so that our endeavours can succeed.'

'I like drawing you out, making you talk, but this is not the time for that. I wish to say something myself.'

'Very well. Not here, though. Let's go into that room at the back.'

They moved into another room, half in darkness with its curtains drawn. It had an old table, flanked by a bench on either side. On the wall was a large map of Bharatvarsha.

'You are doing something unjust. I can't help but point it out.'

Only Ela could address Indranath with such bluntness. Still, even for her, it was not an easy task. So, she spoke with more force than necessary.

It would be inadequate to describe Indranath as handsome. His appearance had a rugged magnetism, as if deep in his heart, he carried a thunderbolt, its roar inaudible to the normal ear but its cruel fire flashing out on occasion. In his expression, a polished urbanity, its sheen like a sharpened knife. He did not hesitate to say harsh things, but he said them with a smile. His voice did not rise when he was angry; instead, his anger manifested itself in a smile. He neither forgot, nor exceeded, the precise restraints that preserved his dignity. Hair close-cropped with no fear of disarray even though he did not take proper care of it. Complexion wheatish, with a ruddy tinge. Above his eyebrows, a broad, high forehead. In his gaze, a hard intelligence. In the set of his lips, the arrogance of firm resolve. He could make the most outrageous demands, knowing that they would not be easily ignored. Some considered his intelligence to be exceptional, others believed that his powers were superhuman. Consequently, he evoked boundless esteem in some and irrational terror in others.

'What injustice?' smiled Indranath.

'You have ordered Uma to get married, but she doesn't want to.'

'Who says she doesn't?'

'She says so herself.'

'Maybe she doesn't know for sure herself, or perhaps she isn't being quite truthful.'

'She had taken a vow in your presence, not to marry.'

'That was true at the time, but not anymore. Truth can't be conjured up with the words we utter. Uma would have broken that vow herself. I am forcing her to break it now, saving her from committing that offence herself.'

'Keeping or breaking the vow is her responsibility. What would it matter if she had broken it herself, committed an offence?'

'In the process of breaking it, she would have destroyed a lot else besides. It would have harmed all of us.'

'But she's shedding a lot of tears over this.'

'In that case, I won't prolong her grief. To put an end to it, the wedding will be held within the next couple of days.'

'But beyond the next couple of days, the rest of her whole life lies ahead!'

'The tears women shed before their wedding raise a false alarm, like the rumbling of clouds at dawn.'

'You are cruel!'

'Because the deity who loves humans is cruel. He favours the bestial.'

'You know that Uma loves Sukumar.'

'That's why I want to separate her from him.'

'Is that her punishment for falling in love?'

'Punishment for falling in love would be meaningless. One may as well mete out punishments for contracting smallpox too. If someone gets the pox, it's better to send them away from home to a hospital.'

'Why not marry her off to Sukumar?'

'Sukumar hasn't committed any offence, after all. How many boys like him do we have amongst our group?'

'What if he agrees to marry Uma of his own accord?'

'Not impossible. Hence the hurry. It is easy for women to lead such high-thinking men astray. It would take just a few tears to convince Sukumar that what he thought was courtesy was actually encouragement. Do my words make you angry?'

'Why would I feel angry? Women signalling encouragement through silent wiles, leaving men to bear the responsibility—there is no lack of such instances in my own experience. It's time to judge these things truthfully. Because I do so, women can't stand me. What does Bhogilal—the one Uma has been ordered to marry—have to say?'

'That utterly good-natured individual doesn't have any opinions to trouble his mind. He considers all Bengali women to be exquisite creations of the Maker. It is necessary to consign such a naïve, moonstruck youth to the periphery of our party. Marriage provides the best dustbin for disposing of such garbage.'

'Then why have you brought women and men together despite the risk of such complications?'

'Because nothing worthwhile can be accomplished by ascetics who have consigned the body to ashes and impotent individuals who have burnt their sexual passions to cinders. When I see any fire-worshippers in our own team carelessly setting their inner selves aflame, I'll eliminate them. Our conflagration is intended to set the entire nation on fire. It cannot be lit by a mind that is extinguished, nor by those who don't know how to suppress the fire.'

Ela sat still, her expression grave. Then she dropped her eyes.

'In that case, please let me go,' she pronounced.

'Why ask me to do something so damaging?'

'You have no idea what I am like.'

'Who says I don't know? One day, your homespun khadi fabric seemed to have acquired a tinge of colour. The sun had risen in your heart—that much was obvious to see. I can sense that your ears await the sound of a particular footstep. Last Friday, when I came to your room, you thought I was someone else. I noticed that it took some time for you to compose yourself. Don't feel embarrassed. There's nothing improper about this.'

Ela lapsed into silence, blushing to her eartips.

'You've fallen in love with someone, right?' Indranath persisted. 'Your heart is not made of dead stone, after all. I also know whom you love. There's no cause for contrition that I can see.'

'You spoke of single-minded devotion to our mission. That may not be possible in every situation.'

'It's indeed not possible for all and sundry. But you are not the kind of woman whose devotion to the cause can be dragged down by the weight of love.'

'But . . .'

'No buts here. There is no letting you off.'

'But I'm of no real use to all of you. You know that.'

'I don't want any work from you. I haven't even told you all about our work. How can you understand what fire you light in the young men's hearts when you mark their foreheads with red sandalwood paste? To ignore that and make you do routine work for a sparse salary will not produce the intended effect. We are not ascetics who renounce the desire for wealth and women. Where wealth is effective, we don't disdain it, and where women have influence, we place them on a pedestal.'

'I shan't lie to you. I realize that my love grows steadily, overtaking all the other things I love.'

'Have no fear. Love with your whole heart. Those who hail the country as the Mother are eternal infants. The nation is not the mother of over-aged infants. Rather, the nation is half-man, half-woman—the deity Ardhanariswar. We can attain nationhood only through the union of men and women. Don't rob this union of its power by confining it in the cage of domesticity.'

'But then, what you've told Uma . . .'

'Uma and Kalu! How will they bear the brunt of love in its harsh, violent aspect? Before it's too late, I'm sending the two of them on a pilgrimage—to the Ganga shore of marriage, the riverside cremation ground where the last rites of all their struggles will be performed. But leave those matters aside. We hear a robber entered your home two nights ago?'

'Yes, he did.'

'Did your training in jiujitsu prove effective?'

'I broke the dacoit's wrist, I believe.'

'Didn't your heart wince and cry out against the violence?'

'It would have, but I was afraid he would violate me. If pain had stopped him, I wouldn't have been able to deliver the final wrench to his wrist.'

'Did you recognize him?'

'I couldn't see in the dark.'

'If you could, you'd have known it was Anadi.'

'Oh no! Our own Anadi! A mere child!'

'It was I who sent him.'

'You! Why did you do such a thing?'

'To test you, and him as well.'

'How cruel!'

'I was there in the room downstairs. I reset the dislocated bone immediately. You consider yourself squeamish when it comes to violence, but I wanted you to realize that squeamishness in the face of danger is not natural. The other day, I asked you to shoot a goat, a mere kid. You said you simply couldn't do it. Your paternal cousin fired the pistol in a show of bravado. Seeing the creature collapse, its leg shattered, she let out a guffaw to flaunt her toughness. That was hysteria. She couldn't sleep all night. But if a tiger was about to pounce on you and you weren't a coward, you would have killed it instantly without hesitation. Seeing the tiger clearly before us in our mind's eye, we have sacrificed all our kindness and sensitivity. Otherwise, we would despise ourselves for being sentimental. That is precisely what Sri Krishna had explained to Arjuna—don't be cruel, but when it comes to duty, you have to be pitiless. Do you understand?'

'I understand.'

'If so, I have a question. Do you love Atin?'

Ela remained silent.

'Should he ever put all of us in danger, will you be able to kill him with your own hands?'

'Such an act would be so impossible for him that I won't hesitate to say yes.'

'And if at all such a thing should become possible?'

'Whatever I might say now, can I ever know my real self?'

'You must get to know yourself. Every day, you must imagine all the terrible possibilities, to keep yourself in a state of readiness.'

'I say with certainty that in choosing me, you have made a mistake.'

'I know with certainty that I am not mistaken.'

'Mastermoshai, I beseech you, please release Atin from this bondage.'

'Who am I to release him? He has tied himself up in knots by his own resolve. His mind will never become free of ambivalence. His sensibility will be assaulted at every moment but his self-respect will nonetheless drag him onwards to the end.'

'Are you never wrong about people?'

'It can happen. There are many people with dual strands woven into their very nature. The two strands don't match. Yet both are real. Such people are often wrong, even about themselves.'

'Are you there, bhai?' a heavy voice called from outside.

'Is that Kanai? Come in, come in.'

Kanai Gupta stepped into the room. A short, stout, middle-aged man. Thorny looking face, unshaven for a week. Receding hairline. A thick khadi wrap above his dhoti, missing the attentions of the laundryman. No shirt. Arms rather short in proportion to the rest of his body, looking as if they were always at work. Kanai's teashop existed primarily to provide food and sustenance to the team members.

'Bhai, you are known for your sage-like verbal restraint,' said Kanai in his customary low, hoarse voice. 'It seems Ela di has ruined that reputation.'

'It is our endeavour to not speak at all,' replied Indranath. 'But exceptions are required to prove the rule. This girl doesn't talk, but gives others the space to air their views—a precious form of hospitality to speech.'

'What's this you say, bhai? Ela di, silent! In your presence she stays quiet, but where she opens her mouth, we encounter a flood of words! I'm advanced in years, but the instant I hear her voice, I rush to eavesdrop on what she is saying, abandoning my notebooks and papers. Now you must pay me some attention. I don't have a voice like Ela di's, but what I tell you very concisely will pierce your heart.'

Ela sprang to her feet.

'A word before you leave,' Indranath said to her. 'To the members of our group, I have criticized you. In fact, I've even said that one day we might have to remove you from the scene without leaving any trace. I've told them that you are inducing Atin to break away from us and that in the process, other things will also be broken.'

'Why repeat those words so often that they actually become a reality? Who knows—maybe there is some mismatch between the set-up here and my own self?'

'In spite of that, I don't suspect you. But still, in the presence of the boys, I criticize you. They say you have no enemies, but I can see that seventy-five per cent of your Bengali devotees are eager to believe these aspersions against you. Such people, who thrive on malice, are feckless. I note down their names. They fill many pages of my notebook.'

'Mastermoshai, they indulge in gossip because they love gossip, not because they harbour any anger against me.'

'You are aware of the name Ajatashatru—the one who has no enemies. But these people are jatashatru—born enemies of their own people. Their irrational hostility, instilled at birth, demolishes all our attempts to reclaim Bengal.'

'Bhai, that's enough for today,' Kanai interjected. 'The matter can be settled the next time. Ela di, if I have been secretly responsible for disrupting your tea party, please don't mind. It is almost time to close down my teashop. Now I'll probably have to set up a barber shop three hundred miles away. Meanwhile, I have prepared five barrels of Alakananda oil, wrung out of Lord Mahadeva's tangled locks. My dear child, please certify in my name, that ever since you started applying Alakananda oil, braiding your hair has become a problem, because managing such luxuriant tresses would be impossible even for the ten-armed goddess Durga herself!'

On her way out, Ela paused at the doorway and turned.

'Mastermoshai,' she said, 'I shall remember your words and remain prepared. The day might come when I will have to be removed from the scene. Then I shall vanish soundlessly.'

'Why do you appear agitated, Kanai?' asked Indranath after Ela had left.

'Recently, sitting at that roadside table right in front of us, some ruffianly boys—perhaps three in number—were expounding on the importance of valour. From the racket they created, you could tell they were John Bull's pets. I've reported their names to the police together with proof of their sedition.'

'I hope you were not mistaken in your assessment, Kanai?'

'Better to harbour mistaken suspicions. More disastrous by far, to mistakenly consider someone above suspicion. If they are real simpletons, nobody can save them and if they are real enemies, nobody can destroy them. Either way, my report can only improve the state of affairs. The other day, they were loudly proposing to unleash a bloody deluge upon the diabolical administrative system. They must have been picked up by the authorities. One evening, I had settled down to balance accounts, when suddenly a youth in ragged, dusty garb came up to me and whispered, "I need twenty-five rupees to go to Dinajpur." He named our Mathu's uncle. "You devil! How dare you?" I yelled, jumping to my feet. "I'll hand you over to the police straightaway." I didn't have the time to spare, or else I would have carried out my practical joke and hauled him to the thana. All those boys of yours, drinking tea in the adjoining room, were furious with me. Trying to collect funds for that fellow, they found that after emptying all their pockets, thirteen annas was all that they could raise. Meanwhile, after his encounter with me, that boy has made himself scarce.'

'So, it seems your cooking vessel is not airtight. The aroma has escaped through a hole in the lid, and now the flies have started arriving.'

'No doubt about that. Scatter your boys far and wide, bhai. Do it right away. Make sure not one of them is jobless. Each of them must have an ostensible means of livelihood.'

'They must indeed. But have you figured out a way?'

'Long ago. My hands were tied, so I couldn't carry it out myself. I've devised a plan and gradually put together the ingredients for it as well. Madhav manufactures jwarashani pills, laced with seventy-five per cent quinine, meant to ward off the malign influence of Saturn. I'll get them from him and re-label them as malaria pills. A lot of lies to load the quinine with. We can deploy Pratul Sen to promote the pills, carrying them around in a canvas tote bag. Your boy Nibaran has a first-class M.Sc. degree. Let him shed his inhibitions and peddle the bhairavi amulet instead. Combining the seven traditional metals with the names of some new metals produced by modern chemistry, our amulet can signal an unprecedented fusion of ancient wisdom with modern science. Let Jagabandhu combine a special turn of phrase with Sanskrit shlokas to proclaim that I hail from the birthplace of Chanakya, from the very same subdivision of Netrakona in Bengal. Let a literary controversy erupt. Ultimately, the annual Chanakya festival can be celebrated on the ruins of my own ancestral property. Let your Tarini Sandel, the doctor from the Campbell School of Medicine, roam the neighbourhood, clamouring for subscriptions to create a temple dedicated to Ma Sitala, the Goddess of Smallpox. The real point is, we must send your stalwarts—the best grenadiers—underground, letting them operate under cover of some fake occupations. Although some will call them idiots, others identify them as shrewd materialists.'

'Your words make me yearn to take up some trade myself,' laughed Indranath. 'For no other reason but to educate myself in the process and psychology of bankruptcy.'

'Bhai, the trade you've taken up will surely lead to bankruptcy, if not today, then tomorrow,' Kanai retorted. 'People don't go bankrupt due to obtuseness but because they can't resist the path to ruin. The death wish for bankruptcy holds out a sublime attraction. No use discussing that subject now. Let me ask a question. You rarely come across a woman as beautiful as Ela, right?'

'Right, indeed.'

'Then what gives you the courage to place her in the midst of your team?'

'Kanai, you should have understood me by now. One who fears the flames cannot play with fire. I don't want to exclude fire from my work.'

'In other words, you don't give a damn whether that destroys your work or not.'

'The Creator plays with fire. The process of Creation doesn't depend on calculating the consequences. It is inspired by the desire for uncertainty. Not for me the covetous mentality that calculates the market price of dolls made of cold clay thumbed into shape. That boy Atin, drawn to us by Ela's magnetism, has explosive dynamite inside him. That's why I take such keen interest in him.'

'Bhai, in this terrible laboratory of yours, we merely perform the role of attendants who sweep and clean. Should some gas catch fire or some equipment explode, our future prospects will shatter. We don't have the brains inside our skulls to take pride in such a scenario.'

'Why don't you resign and leave?'

'We're greedy for the outcome after all, even if you are not. Once, I had heard your agents say that we might find the Elixir of Life. Caught in the trap of your nefarious research, we poor wretches have only succumbed due to our attraction to optimism—that's for sure. You view this as a gamble, but we see it in plain terms, as a trade. Don't end up mocking us, bhai, by setting the account books on fire. Every coin in that account is stained with our life-blood.'

'My mind has no place for superstition, Kanai. I've completely given up all thought of winning or losing. Master of a vast field of endeavour—I occupy this position because it is appropriate. Here, defeat is great and so is victory. They had tried to cut me down to size, closing all the doors around me. Even with my dying breath, I want to prove my greatness. Hearing my call, so many men worth their names have defied death to rush to my side from all directions. You can see that for yourself, Kanai. Why did that happen? Because I know how to summon people. That is a truth I will fully actualize and let others know about it too. Afterwards, come what may. After all, even you appeared to be outwardly ordinary once. It was I who brought your extraordinariness to light. I brought zest into your lives. That's my experiment in human chemistry. What more does one need? A historical epic may conclude in the vast cremation ground of defeat, but it remains an epic still. In this enslaved land of stunted humanity, even the chance to die a worthwhile death is an opportunity.'

'Bhai, you have dragged even a profoundly unimaginative, practical man like me on to the stage where the wildest tandava—the cosmic dance of madness and destruction—is performed. When I think about it, I can't fathom this mystery.'

'It's because I don't beg like a destitute that I can exert such power over all of you. I don't lure anyone with illusions or temptations. I summon them to the scene of impossibility, not to achieve results, but to prove their valour. My nature is impersonal. I can accept the inevitable without agitation. I have studied history and discovered how many great empires attained the zenith of glory only to be reduced to dust. Somewhere in their account books, a huge debt had piled up which they had failed to repay. This land is my own. How can I be so foolish or whimsical as to urge our land to cling to the high throne of history, convinced that good fortune is permanent while ostentatiously offering worship at the shrine of that very cause of our own downfall? I never do that. With the detachment of a scientist, I accept that those who are moribund will die.'

'What then?'

'What then! The dire predicament of the country cannot bow me down. I am far beyond that as well. I will not let my spirit flag, even after witnessing all the symptoms of death.'

'And what about us?'

'Are you young greenhorns? Can you, with all your tears and lamentations, all your prayers to the Lord, rescue a ship whose hull is riddled with holes?'

'And if we can't, what then?'

'What then? Some of you have knowingly raised the deadly sails of that sinking ship in the face of a storm without any qualms. Our victory, even as we sink, rests with such people—as many as we can find. On the mast of a land blindly preparing to sink into the netherworld, you all have raised the flag of ultimate victory. You have not harboured false hope, begged like destitute, or wept and howled in despair. Even when the ship's hull has filled with water, you haven't given up. In surrender lies cowardice. It's done! My mission is complete, thanks to the few like you that I have found. And what lies ahead? *Karmanyewadhikaraste ma phaleshu kadachan.* You have the right to action, not to the fruits of action.'

'It seems to me that you have left out something of major importance.'

'What's that?'

'Do you feel no rage in your heart as well? Are you indeed so impersonal?'

'Rage? Against whom?'

'Against the British.'

'I despise the rustic soldier who can't fight until his eyes become bloodshot with liquor. Trying to do one's duty in a state of anger is more likely to lead to misdeeds.'

'Still, to feel no anger when there is cause for anger sounds inhuman.'

'The whole of Europe is familiar to me. I know the British too. They are the greatest of all the Western races. It's not as if they are incapable of killing when threatened by the enemy, but they can't go all the way—they balk at the prospect. Their greatest fear is having to justify their actions to their own leaders. They delude themselves and also their leaders. I can't muster up the degree of rage necessary to go full steam ahead.'

'You're a peculiar man, indeed!'

'They could have smashed our spines forever by the brunt of a full-scale beating. I laud their humaneness because they didn't do that. While reigning over a foreign land, that humaneness has been worn down. That is what makes them moribund from within. No other race bears the burden of so many foreign lands to dominate. It is destroying their nature.'

'That's for them to deal with. But it seems to me rather extreme that you should take up this endeavour virtually without any objectives.'

'You are utterly mistaken. I will not make an unjust judgement, lose my reason, work myself up into a frenzy by hailing my country as a goddess, calling her "Ma", and shedding copious tears. But still, I will keep on working. That is my strength.'

'If you don't hate your enemy for being the enemy, how can you raise your hand against them?'

'With unperturbed intelligence, just as I would wield my weapon against a stone that blocks my way. Whether they are good or evil is not the question. Their rule is foreign rule. It is destroying our identity from within. In trying to shake off this unnatural predicament, I acknowledge my humanity.'

'But you have no sure hope of success!'

'Maybe not, but what of that? I will not allow my innate nature to be insulted. Not even if impending death is the greatest certainty. It's because there is the danger of defeat that one must sustain one's self-respect by showing the daring how to disregard the possibility of defeat. Indeed, I feel that that is precisely our ultimate duty now.'

'Here comes the false Bhagirath whose mission is to unleash a river of blood. Let me go and offer him tea. And along with that, I'll also give him the clear message that everything has been reported to the police. I hope the idiots in your team will not end up lynching me!'

2

Ensconced in a chair, her back propped up by a cushion, Ela was writing intently with her knees crossed. An open exercise book with Deshbandhu's image on its cover lay at an angle on a wooden board on her lap. It was almost sunset, but her hair was still tousled, unbound. She wore a purple khadi sari, its folds concealing the soiled texture of the fabric. Clearly it was a functional, uncared-for necessity for private use. On her wrists, a pair of shankhas painted red, and around her neck, a gold chain. Her body, pale as ivory, looked firm and trim. She appeared young, but her face had the gravity of mature intelligence. At one end of the room, against the wall, stood an iron bed with a green khadi coverlet. Spread on the floor, a handloom shatarancha mat of the Narayani school . . . Beside it, on a small writing table, a blotting pad flanked by an inkstand and pens, and gandharaj flowers in a brass vase. Hanging on the wall, a ghostly photograph from some bygone age, its faded yellowing lines barely visible. It was growing dark, time to turn on the lamps. Ela was about to arise, when Atin swept in like a gust of wind, flinging the khadi curtain aside.

'Eli!' he called out.

'How uncivilized!' cried Ela, startled but pleased. 'How dare you enter this room without announcing your presence?'

Atin knelt at Ela's feet.

'Life is very short,' he said, 'And manners and etiquette very long drawn out. Ancients of the golden age had a sacred lifespan, time enough to observe all those rules. Now, in Kaliyuga—the last of the four ages—in this modern era headed for the apocalypse, we are racing against time.'

'I haven't dressed yet.'

'All the better. You will match my appearance, then. For you to ride a chariot while I remain a pedestrian—such contraries are against Manu's law. I was a bhadralok once, a perfect gentleman. You're the one who has removed that veneer. Do you notice my current attire?'

'The lexicon doesn't describe such garb as "attire."'

'What do they call it, then?'

'I can't find the words. Maybe they don't exist in the lexicon. That jagged tear right in front of your upper garment—is it a big advertisement of your own needlework?'

'I take the assaults of fate straight on my chest, no matter how terrible they might be. The tear is evidence of that. I dare not give this kurta to a tailor for mending. He has some self-respect after all.'

'Why didn't you give it to me?'

'You've taken on the burden of mending the ways of the new age. How can one add to that the burden of mending an old kurta?'

'What is the need to suffer that kurta?'

'The same need that makes a bhadra gentleman suffer his wife.'

'Meaning?'

'Meaning, one puts up with something when it is the only one available.'

'What's this, Antu! Have you no other clothes in all the world?'

'It's wrong to exaggerate, so I erred on the side of understatement. In an earlier stage of life, Sri Atindrababu's wardrobe was extensive and varied. And then came the flood. In your lecture, you said that in these tear-drenched evil days (do you remember the adjective "tear-drenched"?), when many men and women don't have enough cloth to preserve their modesty, it's the people with surplus clothing who should feel ashamed. You had put that quite eloquently. I didn't have the courage to mock you openly at the time, so I had mocked you in secret. I knew for sure that you had surplus clothes in your wardrobe. But a woman, even if she owns fifty garments in fifty shades, considers all fifty to be absolutely essential. On that occasion, after your speech, female patriots vied with each other to extract the largest donations. I brought my trunk full of clothes to submit at your sacred feet. You applauded in delight.'

'You don't say! How could I have known that you would surrender all you had?'

'Why does that surprise you? After all, who gave my body the instant, invincible power to withstand such an impossible loss? If our Ganesh Majumdar had been vested with the responsibility for collecting donations in this instance, his virility would have made scarcely a dent in the contents of my clothes trunk.'

'Chhi chhi, what a shame, Antu! But why didn't you tell me?'

'Don't upset yourself. My plight is not utterly deplorable. I dyed and kept aside two garments for my daily needs. I wash and wear them alternately. And there are two more, folded away for use in emergencies. In this suspicion-ridden world, if it ever becomes necessary to prove that I am of bhadra descent, those two kurtas will bear the hallmark of the tailor and the laundryman.'

'Your countenance has the Creator's hallmark stamped on it. No need for you to summon up witnesses.'

'Such ardent praise from you! Men have held the eternal birthright to mouth hyperbolic words of praise when courting women. Do you want to turn that law upside down?'

'Yes, I do. I want to publicize the increase in women's rights in the modern age. Women don't hesitate to speak the truth now, even about men. In Navya sahitya—our modern literature—I find that the Bengali women characters are eloquent in their own praise. They have usurped the clay sculptor's role of fashioning the images of goddesses. To the talents and glory of their own kind, they add flourishes of literary colour. They enhance their own complexion with artificial cosmetics—colours applied by their own hand, not the Creator's. It embarrasses me. Come, now, let's move to the sitting room.'

'There's enough room here as well. It's not as if I constitute some large assembly all by myself.'

'Very well, then. Tell me what is the very important thing that you had to say.'

'A few lines of verse come suddenly to mind, but I simply can't remember where I've read them. Since morning, I've been groping blindly for the source. So, I came to ask you.'

'Very important matters indeed, I can see. Achchha, go ahead and recite the lines.'

'Just try to recall who composed these lines:

> I saw in your eyes
>   My own ruin.'

'Definitely not the work of a famous poet.'

'Don't you feel you have heard these words before?'

'I recognize the faint trace of a familiar voice. Where are the accompanying lines?'

'I was convinced that the other lines would surface in your mind on their own.'

'If I hear it from your lips, I'm sure I will remember it.'

'Listen, then:

> Month of Chaitra, year's end,
>   reddened by sunset glow.
> I saw in your eyes
>   My own ruin.'

'What lunacy! What has come over you?' Ela struck her forehead.

'My lunacy began from the inauspicious end of that hot Chaitra month. Days that end without reaching their zenith are left circling the horizon of the imagination like ghostly shadows. My union with you will also take place in a wedding chamber of mirages. I have come to summon you there, to ruin your work.'

'To hell with my work,' cried Ela, flinging her writing board and exercise book on the floor. 'Let me light the lamp.'

'No, let it be. The light shows up the visible truth. Let us take the unlit path to the invisible realm. A little less than four years ago, there I was—on the steamer ferry, at the Mokama crossing. Those days, I was clinging to the broken shore of an ancestral property riddled with debt-ridden holes. My body and soul were still tinged with the hues of finer tastes, like sunset-tinted vagabond clouds at the end of day. Sporting a silk panjabi, folded muga shawl on my shoulder, there I sat on a cane chair, alone on the first-class deck. The pages of my cast-off newspaper fluttered here and there. I enjoyed watching them. They reminded me of the wild dance of rumour. And there you were—among the plebeians, a deck passenger braced for the journey. Suddenly, from the dimness behind me, you appeared swiftly to stand right before me. To this very day, I can visualize clearly that brown sari that you wore. Pinned to your hair knot, your sari aanchal billowed in the wind, framing your face. "Why don't you wear khadi?" you had asked me with a false show of candour. Remember?'

'Very clearly. You make your mental pictures speak, but mine remain dumb.'

'Now I shall repeat the story of what happened that day. You must listen.'

'Why would I not listen? My mind wants to return again and again to that day, that point where my new life made its clamorous demand heard . . .'

'At the sound of your voice, my whole body awakened with a jolt. The music of that voice pierced my heart like a ray of light, as if some exquisite bird had dropped from the sky and pounced on my life eternal, snatching it away. If I could have felt enraged at a mere girl's incredible daring, that day's ferryboat would not have hit such a dangerous shore today. I would have spent my days, to the end of my life, on the common thoroughfare of respectable bhadra society. But like a damp matchstick, my heart refused to flare up in anger. Pride is my primary strength. It flashed through my mind that if this girl had not felt attracted to me, she wouldn't have singled me out for such a rebuke. This promotion of khadi was a mere ruse. Tell me, am I right or wrong?'

'Oh, how many times I have told you this! For a long time, I'd been gazing at you from a corner of the deck, oblivious to the possibility that others might notice. In my entire life, that was the most amazing experience—the birth of a lifelong intimacy in a single moment. My heart wondered where he had come from—this person of some utterly different kind, not built to the same measure as those around me. Like a thousand-petalled lotus blooming amidst the stagnant weeds! At once, I secretly vowed that I must draw this rare human being closer, not just to me, but to all of us.'

'It is my misfortune that your personal desire got subsumed under the collective desires of the crowd.'

'I had no choice, Antu. Before they set their eyes on Draupadi, Kunti had told her sons, "Share the prize amongst all of you." Before you appeared on the scene, I took an oath to bow to the nation's commands, swearing that I will not cling to anything as my personal possession. I am bound by my pledge to the nation's cause.'

'Your pledge is against our own innate dharma, and your adherence to the pledge also constitutes a daily rebellion against your own dharma. Breaking the pledge would preserve the truth. You have allowed the party to trample upon a pure desire inspired by the deity of our innermost souls. You must bear the punishment for that.'

'Antu, the punishment knows no limits; it assaults me day and night. Extraordinary good fortune came my way— the kind that is beyond all striving, an unasked-for gift of destiny. But I could not seize it. To suffer such excruciating widowhood despite our hearts having tied the knot! Let no woman be condemned to such a fate. I was trapped within a magic fence, but the moment I set my eyes on you, my heart eagerly urged me to break all barriers. Never could I have imagined such inner tumult. To say that my heart had never been stirred before would be a lie, but I have conquered my heart's restlessness, taking pride in my own power. Gone, now, is that pride of conquest. I have lost my desire for it. Forget about external appearances and look within me. You will find that I have been defeated. You are the hero, and I, your captive.'

'I too have lost to that captive of mine. My defeat is not yet complete. Every moment a new battle breaks out, and at every moment, I suffer defeat.'

'Antu, even when you had appeared to me on that First-Class deck like a remote, extraordinary vision, I had realized that my Third-Class ticket was a shining token of our new, modern aristocracy. Ultimately, you travelled Second Class on the train. In mind and body, I felt strongly attracted to the same class, because of you. In fact, I thought up a clever trick. I imagined that just as the train started moving, I'd jump into your carriage, pretending to have made a mistake during the final rush to board. In the kavya tradition, it's the women who always set out on a tryst. It's because the laws of domesticity forbid such freedom that the poets feel such pity for women. All the random desires of a restless mind spin around in the heart's dark, innermost chamber, banging their heads on the wall. Beyond the veil that screens their private lives, women refuse to admit to these desires. But you have forced me to acknowledge them.'

'Why did you acknowledge those desires?'

'Breaking the silence of womankind, that acknowledgement was the only thing I could offer you. I had nothing else to offer you, after all.'

'Why not?' Atin demanded, suddenly gripping Ela's hand. 'What stopped you from accepting me? Society? The caste divide?'

'Chhi chhi! For shame! Don't even think such things. The barrier was not external; it was within me.'

'You didn't love me enough?'

'This word "enough" means nothing, Antu. If I failed to move a mountain by the strength of my bare hands, don't malign that as weakness. I took a vow that I would not marry. Even if I hadn't, marriage would probably not have been possible.'

'Why not?'

'Don't be angry, Antu. It's because I love you that I feel such hesitation. I have nothing. What can I offer you anyway?'

'You may as well say it clearly.'

'I have said it many times.'

'Say it again. I want us to finish saying all that has to be said today. After this, I shan't ask you again.'

'Didimoni!' someone called from outside.

'What is it Akhil? Come in.'

The boy was about sixteen to eighteen years of age. Mischievous countenance, obstinate and endearing. Shaggy, curly hair, soft dark complexion, bright restless eyes. Dressed in khaki shorts and an unbuttoned waist-length shirt of the same colour, leaving his chest exposed. The pockets of his shorts bulging with his possessions, sundry bits of rubbish. In the breast-pocket, a knife with a strangely shaped blade, its handle made of horn. Sometimes, the boy made toy boats and model airplanes. Recently, he had seen a wind-operated water-wheel at the ayurvedic garden of the Mullick Company. Now, he was trying to create a model of the wheel, cobbled together from biscuit tins and other castaway items. He had cut his finger, now bandaged with a rag. When Ela enquired about it, he refused to answer.

Ela was this orphaned boy's distant relative. She put up with many of his antics. Akhil had bought a diminutive monkey from someone at a throwaway price. The creature was adept at raiding the larder. In Ela's small household, this animal created an enormous nuisance.

As soon as he entered the room, Akhil touched Ela's feet in a quick, awkward gesture of respect. Ela realized that the ritual pronam had some special reason, for devotion didn't come naturally to Akhil.

'Won't you greet your Antu dada with a pronam?' Ela prompted.

Akhil stood stiff and silent, his back turned to Atin. Atin burst into a guffaw.

'Shabash, well done!' he said, slapping Akhil on the back. 'Bow your head if you must, but only to the deity, the one and only. Before this lone and singular goddess, I too bow my head. Now, bhai, don't quarrel with me over the prasad—consecrated food from her hand.'

'Tell me what you came here to say,' Ela urged Akhil.

'Tomorrow is my Ma's death anniversary,' he responded.

'Indeed it is. I had quite forgotten. Do you want to invite anyone for the sraddha ceremony?'

'No, nobody at all.'

'What do you want, then?'

'Three days' leave from my studies.'

'What will you do with those days off?'

'I'll make a cage for rabbits.'

'Not a single rabbit left, so who will you make the cage for?'

'Rabbits can always be imagined. It's making the cage that really matters,' laughed Atin. 'Humans are transient. They come and go. But from the divine Manu to his latest avatars, there are many who have undertaken to build permanent cages for humanity—a task they relish tremendously.'

'Okay Akhil, you may go. Your leave is granted.'

Without another word, Akhil took to his heels.

'I couldn't tame him,' observed Atin. 'Among the antique belongings I was trying to discard was a wristwatch—a supreme treasure for the boys of today. I offered it to him once, but he shook his head and went away. Clearly, matters have come to a head between the two of us. I see signs of a communal clash, an impending Antu-Akhil riot.'

'When it comes to befriending the boys, there's no match for you. Yet you had to submit to this monkey. Why?'

'Between us stands a third party, else he and I would have become an inseparable twosome. Let that be. Now tell me, what is your excuse for casting me aside?'

'Why can't you remember the simple fact that I'm older than you?'

'Because I couldn't forget the simple fact that you are twenty-eight while I happen to be a few months older. Very easy to prove that, because the facts are not inscribed on copper in the ancient indecipherable Brahmi script.'

'My twenty-eight years far outrun your own twenty-eight. In your twenty-eight years, all the lamps of youth

have burned brightly without smoke. Your window still
remains open to the future, to those yet to arrive, yet to be
imagined in our dreams.'

'Eli, you fail to understand my words because you
simply don't want to understand them. For the party, you
have taken a vow that goes against God's truth. That is
why you delude yourself—and me as well—with all sorts of
made-up arguments. Delude me if you will, but don't say
that in my life, the yet-to-arrive, the yet-to-be-imagined
still remains a distant possibility, for it has arrived already.
You are the one. And yet, it has not quite arrived. Will my
window remain open to it forever? From the heart of that
void, will my anguished tones always ring out, crying, "I
want you"? And from the other side, will no response come
my way?'

'How ungrateful! How can you say that there is no
response? I want you, want you, want you! There is nothing
in this world I want more than I want you. But we did not
meet at that auspicious moment when the shubhodrishti
ritual could have sealed our marriage as we looked upon
each other for the first time. How fortunate, though, that
such a thing didn't happen, I still declare!'

'Why? What harm could have come of it?'

'It would have made my life worthwhile, but what does
that matter? You are not like anyone else, after all. You
are great. It is because I remain at a distance that I can see
your brilliance, dazzling as a flash of lightning. It frightens
me to imagine you entangled with someone as ordinary as
myself. For you to become an ordinary, trivial part of my

circumscribed world! How can I make you understand that I must crane my neck to glimpse your full height, towering so far above me? Women's existence revolves around the small details of everyday life. There may be women who use that burden to weigh down the lives of men— even men like yourself. I know how many tragedies such women have caused. I have seen before my own eyes that the clinging parasite vine does not let the tree in the forest grow. Such women seem to believe that it is enough for men to embrace them.'

'Ela, only the one who receives enough knows what it means to have it.'

'I don't want to delude myself, Antu. Nature has humiliated us women from the time of our birth. We enter this world bearing destiny's purpose in our biology, our bodies. With us, we bring the self-produced weapons and magic spells of our creaturely existence. If we know how to use those effectively, we can easily win for ourselves a place on the throne at very little cost. But men have to prove their worth in the field of dedicated endeavour. By a stroke of good fortune, I've had the opportunity to discover what that worth can be. Men are far greater than us.'

'They are only taller.'

'Yes, indeed they are taller. It is only at such a height that the gateway for transcending the limits of nature can be found. Whether or not I have sufficient intelligence, I've been able to humbly surrender myself in devotion by looking up to those exalted heights.'

'No lowly persons disturbed you?'

'They did, indeed. Attracted by us women, those who descend to the baser levels of biology go astray in hideous ways. Even without any particular personal desire or need, we women have united in a common conspiracy to drag men down, using our attire, manners and artful conversation.'

'To delude fools?'

'Yes, dearest, you are fools—all of you! You can be deceived by our simplest charms. That is why we feel so conceited. We have loved fools but still glimpsed sunshine, even at the heights of their base stupidity. Fools have brought us light, and we have worshipped them. We have encountered many vile, filthy, foul-mouthed men, many who are miserly or ugly. Even after rejecting all of them or accepting all their faults, there still remain many others who are not like them. It is those remaining men that one has regarded in a shining light. Many of them will not be remembered by name, and yet they remain great.'

'Eli, your words embarrass me. They make me feel that I ought to contradict you. But they make me feel good too. Yet, when it comes to truth-telling, I can't concede defeat. Today, I will tell you about the signs of cowardice that I have noticed in the men of our land ever since I was a boy—a cowardice that has troubled me time and again. I have seen, among the families of my acquaintances and even in my own family, the intolerable, unjust dominance of the mother-in-law. The oppression inflicted by mothers-in-law in our land is proverbial.'

'Yes, I know that, indeed. I have seen in my own home that the one with inborn weakness becomes the worst enemy of the weak. No one can be more brutal than such a person.'

'Ela, don't let those words of yours lay the grounds for future criticism of your mother-in-law-to-be. One often hears of inhumane torture inflicted on new brides and finds the mother-in-law to be the main villain of the piece. But who gives the mother-in-law the right to inflict unchecked injustice? It's those mothers' boys! Lacking the strength to uphold their wives' dignity in the face of the female oppressor, do such adolescents ever develop the maturity to be ready for marriage? When they do, they become their wives' mollycoddled little boys. It's when men lack true virility that women take to lowly ways and drag them down. Today, I observe that the powerful ones in this land—those who are determined to achieve something— are keen to abandon women. Those effeminate cowards are afraid of women. That is why, in this land of cowards, you have taken a vow against marriage lest some immature soul get perverted by your womanly influence! Real men will achieve their goals only on the strength of real women. In our blood, we carry this divine decree inscribed by the Maker Himself. The man who fails to live up to this decree is not worthy of being called a man. You had the responsibility of testing me. Why didn't you put me on trial?'

'Antu, I could have argued with you, but I shan't, because I know you're summoning up these irrational arguments out of extreme bitterness. You can't get my vow out of your mind.'

'No, I can't forget it. Because you said, men attain great heights and you fear that women will bring them down! Women don't need to attain any heights; they are complete in themselves. But the wretched male who does not attain greatness remains incomplete, and the Maker feels ashamed of him.'

'Antu, even in that incompleteness, we can glimpse the Maker's desire. That is a great desire.'

'Eli, I can't call the Maker's desire great because His imagination is no less in any respect. At the touch of that artistic brush, women's nature has acquired a magical quality. To the entire realm of domesticity, they have brought an aesthetic flavour, expressing what can't be captured in words through colour, music and their own body, soul and spirit. A simple energy is at work here; that's precisely why it is not simple. That gold chain we see encircling your delicate, pearly throat—it didn't require you to memorize the contents of a notebook. Some unfortunate women fail to bring beauty into the realm they inhabit. Such women end up as loud-mouthed housewives flaunting thick gold bangles or housemaids who spend their lives scouring their courtyards. Such unremarkable persons do exist, in countless numbers.'

'I blame the Maker Himself, Antu. Why hasn't he endowed women with the strength to fight? Why must they have to survive through self-denial? When I read in a book that women are far more skilled than men at espionage— that basest of human occupations—I struck my forehead in despair, at the feet of the Maker's idol, and prayed not to ever be reborn as a woman in my future lives. Viewing men through the female gaze, we have been able to discern their virtues and their greatness by ignoring everything else. When I think about our nation, it is those young men, good as gold, who come to mind. They are my nation. If they make mistakes, those are big mistakes. My heart bursts when I think that they didn't find a place in their own home. I am their mother, their sister, their daughter. Thinking such things, my heart brims over. Women educated in English find it hard to identify themselves as servants, but my entire being cries out that I am a servant. In serving all of you, I find my worth. In this devotion lies the supreme value of our love.'

'That's all very well. There are many men to receive that devotion from you. But why me? I can do without devotion. The list of women's relationships that you offered—mother, sister, daughter—leaves out one significant item. The blame for that lies with my own wretched destiny.'

'I know you better than you know yourself, Antu. In the tiny cage of our romance, your wings will grow restless within a couple of days. The few ingredients at our disposal that are fit to satisfy our hunger will one day be exhausted, leaving you only with the dregs. Then you will realize my poverty. So, I've withdrawn all my claims and surrendered you to the nation's cause with all my heart. There, your power would not suffer any embarrassing constraints.'

Atin's eyes blazed as if a painful wound had been struck a blow. He paced Ela's room from end to end, then came and stood before her.

'It's time to utter some harsh truths,' he declared. 'Who are you to surrender me, to the nation or to anyone else, I ask you? You had it in your power to surrender the gift of tenderness—a possession that truly belongs to you. Whether you call it service or a boon, it doesn't matter. If you permit arrogance, I shall be arrogant. If you demand that I come to your door in humility, I can do that too. But today you belittle your own right to offer a gift. You set aside the inner wealth you could have donated from the storehouse of a woman's glory and say instead that you are handing over the nation to me. It is not yours to give! Not yours, not anyone else's. The nation can't be passed around from hand to hand.'

The colour drained from Ela's face.

'What do you mean? I can't quite understand,' she said.

'I say that the ambit of women's glory, even if it seems to be circumscribed, has inner depths that are limitless. It is not a cage. But the space that you had designated as my nest, by giving it the name of the nation—that nation constructed by your party, whatever it may mean to others—that space itself is a cage, at least for me. My own power, because it can't find full expression within that space, falls sick, grows distorted, commits acts of insanity in its attempt to articulate that which is not truly its own. I feel ashamed, yet the door to escape is closed. Don't you know my wings are tattered? My legs are tightly shackled. One had the responsibility to find one's own place in one's own nation on one's own strength. I possessed that strength. Why did you make me forget that?'

'Why did you forget it, Antu?' asked Ela, her voice full of anguish.

'You women have an unfailing ability to make one forget—all of you. Else, I would have been ashamed of having forgotten. I insist a thousand times over that you have the capacity to make me forget myself. If I hadn't forgotten, I would have doubted my own manhood.'

'If that is so, then why are you rebuking me?'

'Why? That's what I am trying to explain. By deluding me, you carry me to your own universe where your own rights prevail. Echoing the words of your own party, you said that you and your small group have determined the only path of duty in the world. Caught in that stone-paved, official path of duty, my life-stream spins in a whirlpool and its waters grow muddy.'

'Official duty?'

'Yes, that Jagannath Ratha—that grand, sacred chariot of your *swadeshi* duty. The one who initiated you into the sacred mantra decreed that your only duty is to hoist a heavy rope onto your shoulders and keep on tugging at it—all of you together—with your eyes closed. Thousands of young men tightened their waistbands, braced themselves and grasped the rope. So many of them fell beneath the chariot wheels; so many were crippled for life. At this juncture, the moment came for the Ratha Yatra—the ceremonial chariot procession—in reverse. The chariot turned around. Broken bones can't be mended. The masses of crippled workers were swept aside, flung down upon the dust-heaps by the roadside. Their confidence in their own power had been so utterly demolished at the very outset that all of them agreed, with great daring, to let themselves be cast in the mould of puppets of the government. When at the pull of the puppeteer's strings everyone began to perform the same dance moves, they thought in amazement, "This is what the dance of power is all about!" When the puppeteer loosens the strings ever so slightly, thousands and thousands of human puppets get eliminated.'

'But Antu, that only happened because many of them began to dance wildly without keeping to the rhythm.'

'They should have known from the start that humans can't dance like puppets for long. You may try to reform human nature, though it takes time. But it's a mistake to imagine that destroying human nature and turning men into puppets will make things easier. Only when one thinks of human beings in terms of their diverse forms of inner power can one understand the truth about them. Had you respected me as such a being, you would have drawn me close, not to your party, but to your heart.'

'Antu, why didn't you humiliate and spurn me right at the beginning? Why did you make me a culprit?'

'That's something I have told you time and again. Very simply, I longed to be one with you. That hunger was impossible to overcome. But the usual route was closed. In desperation, I pledged my life to a crooked path. You were captivated by it. Now I have realized that I must die on the path I have taken. Once that death happens, you will call me back with open arms—call me to your empty heart, day after day, night after night.'

'I beseech you, don't say such things.'

'I speak like an idiot. My words sound romantic. As if a union sans body, sans materiality can be called a union at all! As if your sense of loss and yearning from that moment of separation in the past can recompense even an iota of the cost of today's thwarted union.'

'Today you seem to be possessed by words, Antu.'

'What! Possessed, today? I have been eternally possessed! Even when I was of tender age, still lisping, words were sprouting from the darkness of that silence—so many similes, so many comparisons, so many fragmented utterances! When I came of age and entered the realm of literature, I found the heaped-up ruins of kingdoms and empires, strewn across the paths of history. I saw the shattered armour of heroes lying scattered around; saw the peepul tree growing from cracks in broken victory pillars and centuries of human endeavour lying silent in a heap of dust. I saw the immovable throne of speech lying on the rubbish heap of time. I saw the rolling waves of time, era upon era, grovelling at the feet of that throne. How often I have dreamt that mine too is the mission of decorating the golden pillars of that throne! Your Antu is a man eternally possessed by words. I no longer harbour the hope that you will ever truly understand him. After all, you admitted him into the ranks of the pawns in your party's chess-games!'

Ela left her chair and bowed her head at Atin's feet. He drew her up to sit beside him.

'In my imagination, I have decorated this slender body of yours with words alone. You are the leafy vine that is my life's companion—my ultimate joy, my ultimate grief. An invisible veil envelops me—a veil of words descending from that mythical capital city, the literary Amaravati, and crowding all around me. I am independent, ever-free. This Mastermoshai of yours is aware of that. Why does he trust me still?'

'That is why he trusts you. To unite with everyone, you must come down to a common level, to take your place amidst all and sundry. But it is simply impossible for you to descend to that level. For that very reason, I believe in you. No other woman could have placed so much faith in any man. Had you been an ordinary man, I too would have feared you like an ordinary woman. But with you, I feel fearless.'

'I condemn such fearlessness. Fear would have made you recognize a man's virility. Since you make such tall demands for the nation, why not also make demands for an extraordinary woman such as yourself? A coward—that's what I am! Flouting the prohibitions of rejection, why couldn't I have snatched you away long, long ago, when we still had time? It was due to civility, gentlemanly qualms. But love is barbaric, after all! A barbarity that carves out its own path, pushing aside boulders blocking the way. A wild, natural waterfall, not a stream of tame tap water in a civilized city.'

'Come Antu, let's go inside,' pleaded Ela, springing to her feet.

'You are afraid!' cried Atin, standing up. 'At last, after so long, you begin to feel afraid! I win. In the first flush of youth, I didn't understand women. In my imagination, I kept them at an insurmountable distance and viewed them from afar. But the time of reckoning has announced that I am what all of you desire. In my heart, I am a man— barbaric, wild, uncontrollable. Had I not lost all that time, I'd have confined you right now in a grip with the force of a thunderbolt, making your very ribs ache. I wouldn't have given you time to think; you wouldn't have had the breath left in you for weeping. Like a brute, I would have dragged you towards my chamber. But today, I have arrived at a path as narrow as a razor's edge. No room here for two people to walk side by side.'

'My dear bandit, there's no need for you to snatch me away. Here! Here, take me! Take me!' Ela went to Atin, her eyes shut, arms outstretched. Falling upon his breast, she raised her face to his.

'Oh no!' she exclaimed suddenly, glancing out of the window. 'There! He can see us!'

'What is it?'

'There, at the street corner. It must be Botu. He's heading this way.'

'He knows where to come.'

'At the very sight of him, my entire body cringes. Flesh and fatty slime are the very stuff of his being. The harder I try to elude him, to hold him at arm's length, the closer he gets. Impure—that fellow is impure.'

'I can't stand him, Ela.'

'I often try to calm myself, telling myself that I misjudge him—but I never succeed. The gaze of his bulging eyes seems to insult me from a distance with its greedy touch.'

'Pay no attention to him, Ela. Can't you utterly banish him from your thoughts?'

'Because I fear him, I can't expel him from my mind. I glimpse within him a bestial spirit that resembles a hideous octopus. I feel that one day he might put out eight sticky tentacles from his heart and imprison me in dishonour. As if he is constantly plotting this move. You may laugh it off as an immature feminine anxiety, but this fear possesses me like a ghost. I fear not only for myself, but even more for you. I know his envy hisses at you like a snake.'

'Ela, animals like him don't have courage. They emit a foul odour, which is why nobody wants to tangle with them. But he fears me from the innermost recesses of his heart, not because I am terrifying, but because I belong to a completely different species.'

'Look, Antu, I have anticipated all sorts of sorrows and dangers in life and am prepared to face them. But I just hope I don't fall into his clutches by some stroke of misfortune. Even death would be preferable.'

Ela gripped Antu's hand, as if it was time for him to rescue her. 'You know, Antu, sometimes I imagine dying a terrible death at the hands of some predatory animal. At such times, I tell my deity that it is better to be devoured alive by a tiger or a bear than to be dragged into the slime and swallowed by a crocodile. Let such a thing never come to pass.'

'Does this mean that I belong to the category of tigers and bears?'

'No, dearest, you are my Narasimha—the lion-faced divine avatar. To be killed by your hand will be my liberation. There—listen to those footsteps. He is coming upstairs.'

Atindra went out of the room.

'Not here, Botu!' he called out loudly. 'Come, let's move downstairs to the sitting room.'

'Ela-di . . .' called Botu.

'Ela-di has gone in to change her clothes. Let's go downstairs.'

'Change? So late? It's eight-thirty . . .'

'Yes, yes, I delayed her.'

'I just need a word with her. Five minutes, that's all . . .'

'She has gone to bathe. She said she doesn't want anyone to enter that room.'

'And what about you?'

'I'm the exception.'

Botu sneered openly.

'All of us remained permanently trapped by the rules of common grammar, while you graduated to Aryaprayog— the priestly grammar for the initiated few—almost as soon as you arrived,' he said. 'Exceptions are a slippery refuge, let me tell you. They don't last very long.'

With these words, he ran downstairs.

'Letter for you!' Akhil had arrived on the scene, a little saw dangling from his hand. He had come away from his unfinished act of creation.

'For your teacher, your didimoni?'

'No, it's for you. He asked me to hand it directly to you.'

'Who?'

'I don't know him.' Handing the letter to Atin, Akhil departed immediately.

As soon as he saw the red tinge of the paper, Atin recognized it as a danger signal. Written in code, the letter said: 'Spend no more time at Ela's. Leave at once. Don't tell her anything.'

To disregard the discipline that he had adopted as his duty would go against Atin's own self-respect. He tore the letter into shreds. For a moment, he stood still outside the locked bathroom door. The very next moment, he was gone. From the road, he glanced up once at the first floor. The window was open. From outside, one could see part of an armchair and, upon it, the corner of a cushion upholstered in red–and–yellow striped fabric.

Atin jumped on to a moving tram.

3

Trees and shrubs, jostling cheek by jowl. Light green, yellowish green and brownish green, their tangled foliage creating a dense darkness. A pond, overflowing with layers of scum from rotting bamboo leaves. Skirting the pond, a narrow, winding path, scarred by the wheels of bullock carts. Fences overgrown with ol kochu, ghentu, monosa and, at intervals, ashsheora. Glimpsed through occasional gaps in the fence, tender young rice shoots growing in stagnant water, in fields with boundaries marked by earthen ridges. The path goes down to the steps of the ghaat at the Ganga's edge. A cracked, broken ghaat, paved with the tiny bricks of bygone days, sloping at a crazy angle. The river below has silted and changed course over time. Further downstream, concealed within the forests that line the shore beyond the ghaat, the ruins of an old house. The accursed shade of that building shelters the ghost of a man who murdered his mother a century and a half ago, or so it is said. In a long, long time, no living soul has made the slightest attempt to challenge that ghostly spirit.

The setting for the present scene is the old, abandoned thakurdalan—the hall for prayer ceremonies. In front of it stretches a large courtyard, heaps of moss-grown rubbish scattered across its uneven floor. Further away, at the river's edge, beneath the dark shadow of a peepul tree with shaggy hanging roots, one can see the remains of a temple shrine, parts of a performance stage, the ruins of an old boundary wall and, dragged ashore, a broken boat, its rib-cage exposed.

Here, at the end of the day, Kanai Gupta stepped into the shadowy hall, Atin's present abode. Atin started in surprise, for even Kanai was not supposed to know about his whereabouts.

'What brings you here?'

'I am out on a detective mission,' Kanai responded.

'Please explain the joke.'

'It's no joke. I am merely a supplier of provisions for all of you. When the malign planet Saturn entered the teashop, I took to the road. The evil gaze of Saturn's team shadowed me. Finally, I went and signed up in their register of detectives. To those for whom the only road left open is the one that leads to the Neemtola cremation ghaat, this is the Grand Trunk Road, cutting across the nation's breast all the way from east to west.'

'So, instead of making tea, you've taken to manufacturing news?'

'This trade doesn't thrive on manufactured stuff. One must provide only the pure, unadulterated truth. It's my task to strangle the prey already caught in the trap. They received all but complete information on your man Haren, so I offered the final sprinkling of facts to nail him. He is now in that official pilgrim-shelter run by the government, the dharmashala at Jalpaiguri.'

'So, it's my turn now, I suppose?'

'The hour draws near. Botu has made good progress with the groundwork. The part of the task left to me will allow you a little time. When you lived in your previous quarters, your diary had suddenly gone missing -- remember?'

'Only too well.'

'It was bound to fall into the hands of the police, so I had to steal it.'

'You?'

'Yes. The gods help those who have virtuous intentions. Once, while you were writing, you were forced to leave the room for five minutes due to my own trickery. That was when I pilfered it.'

'You read the whole thing?' Atin struck his forehead in despair.

'Sure I did! It was one-thirty at night by the time I'd finished reading. I'd never dreamt until then that the Bengali language could exude such sharpness and flavour. That diary held secrets, indeed, but not about the British Empire.'

'Was that virtuous of you?'

'As for virtue, I can't comment. You are a litterateur. In the entire notebook, you have revealed no details or even mentioned any names. Just that when it comes to emotions,

the diary exudes such disgust and disrespect that, had it
emanated from the pen of some rejected candidate for a
ministerial position, it would have caused an explosion in
the royal court. Even if Botu had not tangled with you, that
diary alone would have been sufficient to turn your ruling
planets against you.'

'What! You've read the whole thing?'

'Indeed, I have. What can I say, Babaji? If I had a
daughter and if she had inspired such writings from your
pen, I'd have deemed my fatherhood worthwhile. Truth be
told, it is the nation's loss that Indranath Bhai has dragged
you into his party.'

'Do all party members know about this trade of yours?'

'Nobody knows about it.'

'What about Mastermoshai?'

'He is intelligent. He can guess, but hasn't asked me
about it, nor heard anything from me about it.'

'But you've told me about it.'

'That's the amazing thing. If a suspicious sort like myself
was unable to trust anyone, he would die of suffocation.
Being neither thoughtful nor stupid, I didn't maintain a
diary. If I had, I'd have felt relieved to unburden myself by
handing it over to you.'

'Mastermoshai . . .'

'One can supply information to Mastermoshai, but
one can't confide in him. I may be Indranath's chief
minister, but don't imagine for a moment that I know all
about him. There are things concerning him about which
one doesn't even dare to hazard a guess. It's my belief that

when party members fall away from the team, Indranath sweeps them away into the slush heap of the police force, just as he has done with me. A condemnable move, but not sinful. Let me forewarn you: one day, with his help or mine, you will ultimately find yourself in handcuffs. When that happens, don't take it amiss. It was Botu who first informed police intelligence about your moving into this house. So, to outdo him, I had to take a photograph and hand it to them. Now, let me talk about practical things. I give you twenty-four hours. If you remain here beyond that time, I will personally escort you to the thana. Here—I have written down detailed directions to your next destination. The code is familiar to you, but still, tear up this paper as soon as you have memorized its contents. Here, look at this map. You will stay in a corner room of a school building on this side of the street. Right across from the police thana. There is a writer constable on duty there, a distantly-related great-nephew of mine. I call him raghav boal—the monster catfish. Their family moved to the western region three generations ago. You've been assigned the role of a Bengali tutor. The moment you get there, "Raghav" will search your trunk, shake out your pockets, maybe even push and prod you a bit. Take that as a sign of divine mercy. Raghuvir is fond of swearing against Bengalis in Hindi. Don't even try to contradict him. Never return to these parts as long as you live. I'm leaving my bicycle outside. The moment you receive the signal, get on it. Come, babaji! One last hug.' A quick embrace, and Kanai departed.

Atin remained sunk in silence. He began to introspect. The final act of his life had arrived at an untimely hour, the curtain about to descend, the lamp nearly extinguished. The journey had begun in the pure light of dawn, but now he had come a long way from where he started. The resources he had at hand at the outset had been exhausted, and now there was nothing left. During the last part of his journey, he had constantly sustained himself on self-deception. The extraordinary gift offered to him by the goddess of fortune one day, at a sudden bend in the road, had seemed like something out of this world. Until then, he had never imagined it possible that such limitless wealth could come his way; he had only encountered its imaginary form in poems and in history. Time and again he had felt that the two of them, Ela and Atin, were Dante and Beatrice reborn. That historical inspiration spoke eloquently within his heart. Like Dante himself, Atin too had plunged into the whirlpool of revolution. But where was its truth, its heroism, its glory? In no time at all, with inexorable speed, the revolution had dragged him into such a slimy quagmire that the shining column of history could never arise from the darkness of that masked thievery and murderousness. Having consigned his soul to disaster, he finally realized that now there could be no prospect of any noble outcome—only inevitable defeat. Even defeat can have value, but not the defeat of the soul—a defeat that had dragged him into a furtive, hideous horror, meaningless and without end.

The daylight waned. In the courtyard, the chirping of crickets could be heard, and somewhere in the distance, the groan of a moving bullock cart.

Suddenly, Ela rushed into the room blindly, like someone plunging into the water in an impulsive bid to end her life. As Atin sprang to his feet, she flung herself upon his breast.

'Atin, Atin, I couldn't stop myself,' she choked.

Atin slowly extricated himself from her embrace and held her at arm's length. He stared at her tear-stained face.

'Eli, what have you done!'

'I don't know.'

'How did you find out about this address?'

'You didn't share your address,' she responded with grave reproach.

'The one who shared it with you is not your friend.'

'I know that for certain, too. But not knowing where you had gone made my mind spin in empty circles until it became too much to bear. I'm in no state to tell friend from foe. Tell me, how long has it been since I saw you?'

'You are amazing!'

'You are amazing, Antu! When forbidden to visit my house, you were able to accept it, after all.'

'That was my natural pride. A tremendous desire coiled around me like a python, nearly crushing me, but still, I could not obey it. They call me sentimental. People had assumed that when it came to the crunch, I'd prove to be a damp squib. It's beyond their powers to imagine that sentiment itself can be my indomitable strength.'

'Mastermoshai knows that.'

'Eli, ever since it came to be haunted, no Bengali bhadramahila has set foot in this place.'

'That is because no Bengali bhadramahila's destiny has ever confronted her with such an exigency in such intolerable circumstances.'

'But Ela, what you have done today is against the rules.'

'I know it. I admit my weakness. But still, I will break the rules, not only on my behalf, but also on yours. Daily, my heart says that you are calling out to me. My spirit grows desperate because I am not allowed to answer. Say—say you are happy that I have come to you!'

'So happy that I'm ready to face risk and danger, just to prove it.'

'No, no, why should you be at risk? Let me suffer the brunt of whatever might be in store. So let me take your leave, Antu.'

'No way! You have broken the rules to come away, and I shall break the rules to hold you here. Let's share the blame equally, the two of us. Once, I had seen your countenance brightened by the spring hues of a newfound sense of wonder. Now that day has receded into another millennium in history. Let us welcome back that day— here, inside this derelict room. Come, come closer.'

'Wait, let me set this room in some kind of order.'

'Alas, that's like trying to comb a bald pate!'

Ela took a quick look around the place. A blanket had been flung on the floor, and on top of that, a reed mat—a chatai. In place of a pillow, an old canvas bag, stuffed with books. A packing case, used as a makeshift reading desk. In a worn wicker basket, a bunch of bananas, and in their midst, a bowl with chipped enamel, meant for drinking tea, whenever a rare opportunity might present itself. At the other end of the room stood a large, wide safe with a clay statue of Ganesha upon it, proof that someone else—Atin's double—had been there. On a cord stretched across two pillars hung some gamchhas stained in different colours. The dank odour of a choking sky filled the interior of the stifling room.

Ela had witnessed some similar, if not identical, scenes before. They had never caused her so much pain. Rather, in her mind, she had lauded the heroism of those young men, capable of such sacrifice. Once, at the edge of the jungle, she had seen the ashen ruins of a cooking stove fuelled by straw and stubble beneath the ruined ceiling of a space where inexpert hands had attempted to cook rice. It had seemed to her a picture, drawn in burning coal, of a revolutionary romance that had shaken a nation. But today, her voice choked with sorrow. Ela had been accustomed to scorning rich young men wrapped in the embrace of luxury. But her heart simply could not bear to see Atin in such a squalid, wretched, worn-out state of deprivation.

Seeing Ela's anguish, Atin laughed out loud.

'You feel stupefied at my wealth and magnificence,' he joked. 'What amazes you is that most of my wealth is not visible. We have to travel light. When it's time to run, no human being, nor any possessions, can call you back or ask you to linger. Workers in the jute factory live in a slum not far away. They call me Masterbabu and make me read out their mail, address their letters, calculate whether their dues have been properly paid or not. Among them are mothers who dream that their children will rise from the working class to the level of officers. They want my help. They bring me fruits and snacks or some milk if they own a cow.'

'Antu, that safe in the corner over there—who does it belong to?'

'Living alone in the wrong place attracts unwelcome attention. By a stroke of misfortune, a Marwari trader—a vagabond if there was one—turned up in this room. Vagrancy is his prime trade, I suspect. This ruined hall serves as a training academy for two nephews of his. They come here after breakfasting on chhatu at dawn, dye cheap fabric for women, sell it to pay interest on their debts and even manage to repay some of the capital. Those clay basins you see are not my cooking utensils for ritual prayer offerings. They are meant for mixing dye. The men stow the fabric in that safe. It also contains other accessories for women— Bellary bangles, combs, small mirrors, brass armlets. The burden of protecting the stuff rests on me and on the resident ghost. At three in the afternoon, the fellows set forth to sell their goods and don't come back here afterwards. I wonder what trade the Marwaris practice in Kolkata. Tempted to learn English from me, those men had wanted to offer me a partnership in their business, but out of human kindness for other living beings, I didn't agree. They also tried to verify my financial status, but I let it be known that most of the wealth from my ancestral heritage has been reborn in their own ancestral homes.'

'How long are you supposed to stay here?'

'Twenty-four hours, I guess. In that same courtyard, the play of colours, tinged with changing emotions, will continue as before, day after day. But Atindra will vanish into the hazy, distant horizon. I only hope that the Marwari who had come in contact with me does not contract the disease of imprisonment which now rages as an epidemic. It's hard to predict whether or not he might share my fate, even without investing in it as a stakeholder.'

'Your future address?'

'I don't have permission to say.'

'Am I not permitted to even imagine where you might be?'

'What is the harm in imagining things? The shore of Manasarovar—the heavenly lake on Mount Kailash— would be a good location.'

Meanwhile, Ela had taken the books out of the bag and begun inspecting them, turning them over in her hands. There was poetry, some in English, and one or two books in Bengali.

'I have carried those around with me all these days, lest I forget the community to which I belong,' Atin informed her. 'In that realm of utterance was my original habitation. As soon as you open the pages, you will find the streets and lanes of that place charted out in pencil. And now? Look where I am today!'

Suddenly, Ela sank to the floor and clutched his feet.

'Forgive me, Antu, please forgive me,' she pleaded.

'What do I have to forgive you for, Eli? If the Lord exists and has boundless mercy, may He forgive me.'

'When I didn't know you for what you were, I led you to this path, to this place where you stand now.'

'I have arrived at this non-place, driven full steam by the force of my own lunacy,' laughed Atin. 'Won't you at least let me bask in that little bit of fame? I tell you I won't tolerate it if you project me as an immature adolescent and try to assume the role of guardian. Better if you come off the stage, look me in the face and say, "Come, come, my beloved, come and rest on my aanchal, the outspread edge of my sari."'

'I could have said something like that, but why did you lose your temper today?'

'Wouldn't I lose my temper? After all, you said that you have dragged me on to this path by the force of your sacred, lotus-like hands.'

'Why does it anger you if I say what is true?'

'Can that be called the truth? I've been flung on to this path by the force of my inner emotions. You are merely the pretext. Had I found a pretext in a Bengali woman of another type, I would by this time have started playing bridge at the clubs where white and coloured people mingle, and at the horse races, I would have endeavoured to ascend to that celestial place—the Governor's box. If it's proven that I am stupid, then I shall declare with a flourish that the stupidity is my own. What they call God-given brilliance.'

'Antu, no more nonsense, I beg you. I am the one who has ruined your career. That is a regret I shall never shake off. I can see that your life has been severed at the root.'

'At last, the real woman emerges! Revealing that on the stage where the drama of saving the nation is enacted, you play the role of the romantic. You occupy centre stage, palm leaf fan in hand, in that scene of nurture, the kind of household that serves up delicacies such as rice and milk and fish head on a kansha platter. At the scene of political violence and turbulence, you arrive with dishevelled hair and glaring eyes, carried away by your own derangement, not guided by everyday common sense.'

'Antu, how can you even say such things? Even women can't match your verbosity.'

'As if women know how to talk! They just rant. There was a time when storm clouds had gathered in my mind to smash the foundations of pure stupidity with a verbal tornado. You women are out to erect your victory pillars on those very foundations of stupidity, though sheer force.'

'Explain to me, I beseech you—why did you take the wrong path simply because of a mistake I made? Why did you inflict upon yourself the suffering of renouncing your occupation?'

'That is my vyanjana—a gesture, as they call it in English. That is the language of my imminent hour of death. Had I not embraced suffering, you would have turned away from me. You'd never have realized how much I love you. Don't dismiss that and say it was love for the nation.'

'The nation does not figure in all this, Antu.'

'Because my pursuit of the nation has merged with my pursuit of you, the nation does figure in all this. There was a time when one had to win the hand of a woman by proving one's worth through acts of valour. Today, I have got the opportunity to gamble with death in that same way. Forgetting that, you only feel anguish about something so trivial as my lack of a livelihood, goddess Annapurna!'

'We women are worldly. We can't bear to think of material forms of insolvency. You must honour one request of mine. I own my ancestral home and some savings. I beg you, again and again—give me your word that you will not hesitate to accept some funds from me. I know you are in great need of money.'

'If in dire need, various options are open to me— from writing help-books for matriculation examinations to working as a porter.'

'Agreed, Antu. By now, I should have spent all my savings on the cause of the nation. But because we women have few earning opportunities, we have a blind addiction to hoarding. We are cowardly.'

'That is the prompting of your common sense. Women lose their grace when they become impecunious.'

'We live in small nests where we collect some odds and ends. But that is because we need not only to survive, but also to love. Everything I possess is intended for you. If I can make you understand that, I will feel immensely relieved.'

'I shall never understand that. Up until today, women have offered service while men have worked for a living. Should the opposite happen, I must bow my head in shame. What I can seek from you without any hesitation, you have rejected in favour of a vow that acts like a dam between us. The other day, you were adding up accounts in the ledgers of Narayani High School. I came and collapsed beside you, like a storm-hit eagle falling to the ground. I had come to you with a battered spirit. Women's dedication to any random thing that bears the stamp of duty is just like their unshakeable devotion at the feet of a temple priest—it is impossible to tear them away from it. You did not look up. Sitting there, I was gazing at you fixedly, longing for the sweetness of your touch to pour forth from those delicate fingers, all over my body and soul. But you remained utterly unmoved. So miserly of you—you couldn't even give me that! I said to myself, "So, I suppose I must pay an even higher price. One day, I shall collapse on the ground with smashed skull and wounded body. Then, you will lift up my broken soul and hold it close, in your lap."'

Ela's eyes grew moist.

'Oh, there's no arguing with you, Antu!' she said. 'Couldn't you take this small trifle without asking? Why didn't you snatch away my account book? Don't you realize that it's your hesitation that constrains me? Antu, your nature resembles that of women, in one respect. Your desire may be tremendous, but it offends your taste to express its claims impetuously.'

'It's an inherited idea, ingrained since childhood in the very marrow of my bones. I've always believed that women's bodies and souls have a certain dignity arising from their purity. To anxiously protect their physical honour has been our practice through the generations. If ever your heart longs to offer even the slightest encouragement to my diffident spirit, don't wait for me to beg for alms. I have not been trained to ask for things in that fashion. To think I can be greedy because my hunger is boundless is alien to my nature. I can't destroy the distinctive quality of my desire.'

Ela came close to Atin. Drawing his head to her bosom, she leaned her cheek upon it. From time to time, she ran her fingers through his hair. After some time, Atin raised his head and grasped her hand.

'The day I boarded the ferry at Mokama, I didn't realize that the grandmotherly goddess of fortune had come and tweaked my ear with invisible fingers. Since then, my heart has been constantly gathering airy blossoms from the sky of memory. Have the events of that day faded from your heart?'

'Not at all.'

'Listen, then. My Bihari attendant had carried the heavy baggage from the lower deck to the carriage. Carrying a small leather case, I was searching for a coolie. With an air of innocence, you came up to me and asked, "Do you want a coolie? What is the need? I'll carry the stuff." "What's this! What are you doing?" I started protesting, but you had already picked up the bag. Observing my discomfiture, you responded, as if reiterating your suggestion: "If you feel embarrassed, why not pick up that box of mine and carry it? That way, we can settle our mutual debts." I had to pick up your box. It was seven times heavier than my case. Shifting the handle from one hand to the other, I staggered to the train, and heaved the box into the Third Class compartment. By then, my silk panjabi was soaked in sweat. I was panting. You were silently amused. Perhaps some trace of pity lingered within you, but you felt it was not appropriate to express it. That day, the great responsibility of helping me grow to maturity rested in your hands alone.'

'Chhi chhi, how embarrassing! Don't speak of it, don't mention it. I feel ashamed to remember what I was then— how foolish, how bizarre! Because you suppressed your laughter at the time, I became more daring. How did you tolerate it? Don't women need some intelligence, after all?'

'It didn't matter. The circumstances in which you had appeared to me on that occasion had nothing to do with advanced mathematics or logic. It was about enchantment, as they call it. Even a champion thinker like Shankaracharya could not make a dent in that with the blows of his giant intellectual cudgel. It was growing dark then, the clouds blushing like a prospective bride when viewed for the first time. The rippling waters of the Ganga were bathed in that reddish hue. Your slim, agile form, silhouetted against that rosy radiance, became etched in my heart forever. What happened after that? I heard your call. But look where I have arrived now! So far away from you. Do you even know about the train of events that led to this situation?'

'Why don't you tell me, Antu?'

'One has to obey the prohibition. And that's not all, is it? What's the point of telling you everything? . . . The light has faded. Come, come closer. My eyes seek you out, as if appealing to your court for a reprieve. Only you can set me free. What I ask is very small, like a tiny gilt frame. Why not frame your image within it? There, those tendrils of

disobedient hair falling over your eyes, your hands brushing
them upward, your black-bordered tussar sari, no brooch
on your shoulder, the sari aanchal pinned to the hair on
top of your head, eyes shadowed with weary suffering, lips
bearing a hint of pleading and, all around you, the daylight
waning in a final, indistinct haziness. What I see now is
the extraordinary truth. Its meaning is impossible to explain
to anyone. Because it could not be captured in words by
some matchless poet, there is such profound sorrow in its
unexpressed sweetness. Surrounding this minute, exquisite
completeness is the frowning gaze of a monstrous untruth
with a big name, casting an enormous shadow.'

'What's this, Antu!'

'A quantity of lies. I remember you asking me to
take up lodgings in a slum for coolies. In your heart was
the intention of reducing my familial pride to dust. That
large-hearted enterprise of yours amused me. One joined
a democratic picnic. I roamed the colony where drivers
reside. I started forging relationships—as dada or khuro,
elder brother or uncle—as I walked past dairies and buffalo
sheds. But they—and myself as well—didn't take long to
realize that these relationships wouldn't work. There must
be some esteemed individuals who can play along with any
tune, even with the twang of a cotton-gin. But when we
try to ape them, we can't match the tune. Haven't you seen
the disciples of Christ in your neighbourhood clasp all and
sundry to their bosoms, calling them brothers, as if it is part
of their ritual practice to do so? That amounts to a mockery
of Christ.'

'What's the matter with you, Antu? What bitterness
goads you to say such things? Are you saying that duty can't
be accepted as such even after overcoming one's distaste for
it?'

'It's not taste but nature we are talking about, Eli. It was
a hero's duty that Sri Krishna had urged Arjun to perform,
however distasteful it might be. He hadn't asked him to
practice agricultural economics with the aim of ploughing
the field of Kurukshetra.'

'Had you been the addressee, what would Sri Krishna
have said, Antu?'

'He had whispered it to me long ago. It was my
responsibility to speak out and articulate that secret message
of his. But our guru has whispered in our ears that the same
duty is indiscriminately assigned to all. That is why so much
artificiality and falsehood have been generated! I say it to
your face: that locality of theirs where you try to conduct
yourself humbly out of your own pride has no place for
you either. Devis! You are devis—goddesses, all of you!
The artificial attire of fake goddesses, like all other kinds of
female attire, is manufactured in the tailoring shops of men.'

'Look, Antu, even today, I don't understand why you
didn't forcibly turn back, leaving the path that was not
meant for you.'

'Let me explain, then. There were many things I didn't
know, many things I hadn't considered before setting foot
on this path. One by one I saw, close at hand, young men
who, had they not been my juniors in age, would have
deserved my obeisance. What sights they have witnessed,

what torment they have borne, how they have been humiliated—such unbearable things will never be divulged anywhere. That was the unbearable anguish driving me mad. Time and again I vowed to myself not to be defeated by fear or vanquished by torture. I vowed that I would die, smashing my head against that heartless wall of stone, but not stop flaunting my contempt for it.'

'Did you undergo a change of heart after that?'

'Hear me out. One who fights the powerful stands at par with the adversary, even if he has no recourse. That protects his honour—an honour that I too had dreamt of. As the days progressed, it became evident that young men of a rare high-mindedness gradually began to lose their humanity. There can be no greater loss. I knew for sure that they would derisively dismiss my words or mock me in anger, but still, I told them that answering the unjust with injustice amounts to defeat. Before defeat, before dying, we must prove to the world that we are greater than them when it comes to the dharma of humanism. Why else are we playing this losing game against such tremendously mighty forces? Surely not out of suicidal stupidity? Not that all of them failed to understand what I was saying. But how many actually did?'

'Why didn't you leave their company, even at that point?'

'Was it even possible to leave anymore? By then, the cruel net of retribution had started encircling them. I personally witnessed their history, understood their heart-rending agony. So, whether their predicament enrages me or makes me despise them, I still can't abandon those who are in such distress. But one thing I have completely understood through this experience is that if we try to engage in physical combat with those whom we simply cannot match in sheer brute strength, we are bound to suffer a deplorable inner wretchedness as a result. In any body, illness causes suffering, but in a weak body, it is fatal. Those with muscle power can go about beating the victory drum for some time, even after insulting humanity, but we can't do that. Blackened through and through with the stigma of disgrace, we will fade into the darkness of infamy when we arrive at the ultimate point of defeat.'

'For some time now, the shape of this terrible tragedy has become clear to me as well, Antu. I had entered the scene at the call to glory, but with each passing day, my sense of shame has grown. What can we do now? Please tell me.'

'Before every human being lies the struggle for one's dharma on the battlefield of dharma. To die there is, as the saying goes, to attain the supreme heaven—*mrito bapi tena lokatrayam jeetam*. But at least for a few of us, the path to that place is blocked, in this lifetime. We must completely pay for our deeds in this earthly realm itself before we depart.'

'I understand everything. But Antu, of late you have been speaking so contemptuously of our work for the nation that it hurts me profoundly.'

'The reasons for that don't need to be discussed at this point. The time for that is past.'

'Tell me all the same.'

'Today I shall admit to you that I am not the kind of patriot all of you talk about. For those who don't recognize the highest supremacy of that which is greater than patriotism, riding on the idea of patriotism is like climbing on to a crocodile's back, mistaking it for a ferryboat. Falsehood, baseness, mutual distrust, conspiracies for seizing power, espionage—all these things will one day drag them down to the bottom of the cesspool. I can foresee that quite clearly. Breathing the poisonous air of falsehood within the ugly world of that pit can never sustain the energy of manhood that enables one to accomplish any great task on earth.'

'Achchha, Antu, this thing you call suicide—does it happen only in our land?'

'I didn't say that. To claim that one can revive the nation's life by destroying its soul is a terrible lie that nationalists across the world are ready to announce in tones as loud as a wild animal's roar. My heart churns with unbearable anguish at the urge to protest against that claim. I could perhaps have declared my conviction in the language of truth—that would have been a greater eternal truth than attempts to save the nation by playing hide-and-seek inside a tunnel. But in this present life, I didn't get the time to say it. That is why my agony torments me so cruelly today.'

Ela sighed deeply. 'Come back, Antu.'

'The way back is closed now.'

'Why?'

'Even if one arrives at a non-place, there are responsibilities to be met there right to the very end.'

'Come back, Antu,' cried Ela, embracing him. 'You have broken the foundations of the belief in which I had sought refuge all these years. Today, I'm clinging on to a broken boat that drifts aimlessly. Save me, take me along with you! Don't remain so quiet. Speak, Antu—say just one word! Order me now, and I will instantly break my vow. I made a mistake. Forgive me!'

'There is no hope of saving the situation.'

'Why not? There must be a way!'

'The arrow may lose its direction but it can't return to the quiver.'

'I am a swayamvara—a woman who chooses her own husband. Marry me, Antu. We can't waste any more time. Let us have a Gandharva marriage in the age-old tradition—a consensual union without formal rituals. Make me your partner in marriage and take me along with you on the path you must follow.'

'If it was the path to danger, I would have taken you with me. But where dharma has been destroyed, I can't make you my life's companion. Let it be, let such things be. In the final moments of this life, as the boat sinks, there is still some truth left. Let me hear about it from you.'

'What should I say?'

'Say you loved me.'

'Yes, I did.'

'Say you will remember that I loved you even when I am gone.'

Ela remained silent. Tears streamed from her eyes.

'I urge you again, Antu, accept something from me,' she finally pleaded in a choked voice, after a long pause. 'Here, take this necklace of mine.' She placed the necklace at his feet.

'Never!'

'Why? Does it offend you? Are you too proud?'

'Yes. Had you offered it to me in times when such things were possible, I would have worn the necklace like a garland around my neck. But now you want to place it in my pocket—a hollow space of hunger and want. I shan't accept alms from you.'

Ela fell at Atin's feet. 'Take me as your companion,' she pleaded.

'Don't tempt me, Ela. I have told you many times, my path is not for you.'

'Then it is not for you either. Turn back, turn back!'

'The path does not belong to me. I belong to the path. No one calls a noose a necklace.'

'Antu, know this for sure—if you leave, I won't live for a single second. I have nobody but you. Even if you doubt that today, I hope with all my heart that there exists some way for that doubt to be completely wiped out after my death.'

Suddenly, Atin sprang to his feet. From the distance came a piercing whistle, sharp as an arrow. He started.

'I must go!'

Ela flung her arms around him.

'Stay a little longer!'

'No.'

'Where are you going?'

'I know nothing.'

Ela clutched his feet.

'I am your devoted servant,' she declared. 'Don't leave me behind! Don't leave!'

Atin stopped in his tracks for a brief moment. Then came the second whistle.

'Let me go!' Atin roared. He snatched his feet away from her grasp and left.

The darkness of dusk had deepened. Ela lay prone on the floor. Her breast felt dry, her eyes had no tears. Suddenly, she heard a deep, sombre voice calling out to her.

'Ela!'

She sprang to a sitting position. Indranath had entered, flashing an electric torch. She rose to her feet.

'Bring Antu back,' she demanded.

'Let that be. Why did you come here?'

'Because I knew it was dangerous.'

'Who cares about any danger to you?' said Indranath in a tone of sharp rebuke. 'Who gave you news of this location?'

'Botu.'

'And still you didn't understand his intent?'

'I didn't have the wits left to understand. My heart was suffocating.'

'I'd kill you this instant if I could. Get back home. There's a taxi waiting outside.'

4

'You again, Akhil! Absconding from boarding school! There's no way of managing you. How many times have I warned you not to visit this house under any circumstances? It'll be the death of you.'

Akhil did not respond to Ela's expostulations. Instead, lowering his voice, he informed her, 'Some bearded fellow has jumped over the rear wall and entered the garden. So I'm locking the door to this room of yours from within . . . Listen! You can hear his footsteps.'

Flicking open the broadest blade of his penknife, Akhil lay in wait.

'Have no fear!' called a voice from the staircase. 'This is Antu here.'

In an instant, Ela's face turned ashen.

'Open the door,' she instructed.

Akhil opened the door. 'Where is that bearded man?' he demanded.

'The beard is sure to be found in the garden. The rest of the man can be found right here. Go, hunt for that beard.'

Akhil left the scene.

For a few seconds, Ela stood gazing at him transfixed, like a stone statue.

'Antu, why do you look such a sight?'

'Not captivating, for sure,' said Atin.

'Is it true, then?'

'What is true?'

'That you have caught some dreaded disease?'

'Doctors have conflicting views. One may as well not believe them.'

'I'm sure you haven't eaten anything?'

'Let that be. Don't waste time.'

'Why did you come here, Antu? Why? They're waiting to capture you, after all.'

'I don't want to disappoint them.'

'Why did you come here, courting trouble?' Ela gripped his arm. 'What's to be done now?'

'Just before I depart, I'll tell you why I came here. And then I'll leave at once. Meanwhile, for as long as possible, that is the very thing I want to forget. Let me lock the doors downstairs.'

He came back upstairs after some time.

'Let's go up to the terrace,' he proposed. 'I've removed all the lightbulbs downstairs. Don't be frightened.'

They climbed up to the terrace, the two of them, and locked the door. Atin reclined against the locked door. Ela sat facing him.

'Relax, Ela. Let's pretend nothing has happened, as if
the two of us are still in the Sundar Kanda phase of the
Ramayana, before the start of the Lanka Kanda where all is
destroyed. Why are your hands ice cold? They're trembling!
Here, let me warm them.'

Atin clasped Ela's hands close to his chest beneath
his shirt. From somewhere far away, the strains of a
shehnai wafted across from some wedding venue in the
neighbourhood.

'Are you frightened, Eli?'

'What is there to be frightened of?'

'Everything. Every moment.'

'I fear for you Antu, not for anything else.'

'Eli,' Atin urged, 'try to imagine us here, in this place,
on just such a silent night, fifty or a hundred years hence.
The limits of the immediate present are extremely narrow.
Within them, fears, anxieties, sorrow, suffering—all these
things seem to loom very large in a false, exaggerated
fashion. The present is a base element which tries to utter
things that are too big for its small voice. It wears a mask
to frighten us, as if we are infants to be momentarily
dandled on its lap. Death tears off that mask. Death doesn't
exaggerate. What I deeply desired had an exorbitant price
marked on it by the lying present. The loss I feel most
profoundly is labelled with a price tag marked in temporary
ink by limitless grief. All lies! Life is a fraud. It wants to
forge the signature of eternity, to pass itself off as genuine.
Death comes to laugh at this deception, erasing the false
document. Death's laughter is not cruel, nor does it mock

us. It is calm and beautiful, like the smile of Shiva after dispelling the night of illusion. Eli, alone at night, have you ever felt the tender, profound freedom of death bearing within itself eternal forgiveness ?'

'I don't have your ability to see the big picture, Antu. But when my heart is overwhelmed with anxiety thinking about all of you, I try very determinedly to convince myself that dying is easy.'

'You coward! Why do you consider death an escape route? Death is the greatest certainty. In it lies the ocean that is the supreme destination towards which all the streams of life flow. The final merging of all truth and untruth, good and evil, takes place in death. Tonight, at this very moment, the two of us are enclosed within the embrace of the outstretched arms of that vast reality. Ibsen's lines come to mind:

Upwards
Towards the peaks,
Towards the stars,
Towards the vast silence.'

Ela remained silent, clasping Atin's hand in her lap. Suddenly, Atin broke into a guffaw.

'Behind us, in the eternal realm, the curtain of death remains closed, utterly still. And against it, the comic drama of life is dancing its way towards the final act. Now, look upon an image of that very performance. Three years ago, on this date, on this very terrace, you had celebrated my birthday, remember?'

'I remember it only too well.'

'Your entire gang of devoted young men had turned up. The food was not lavish. You had served fried chirey—parched rice—with boiled peas, sprinkled with chilli powder. There were also some egg fritters, I recall. Everyone snatched up and devoured the food. Suddenly, Motilal began to declaim, gesticulating wildly, "It's a new birth for Atinbabu today . . ." I jumped up and clamped my hand over his mouth to silence him. "If you start giving public speeches, that's the end of your own previous birthdays," I said. Botu chimed in, "Chhi, chhi, for shame Atinbabu! Killing a speech in the embryo?" . . . New age, new birth, gateway of death and suchlike—their formulaic catchphrases make me cringe. They were trying with all their might to paint my heart with their party's brush, but the colour just didn't take.'

'How stupid of me, Antu! It was I who had imagined that I would draw you in, to make you blend in with all our foot soldiers by dressing you in the same uniform.'

'That is why, for my benefit, you used to play the didi to the hilt with all of them. You had imagined it necessary to arouse some jealousy, to reform the faults in my character and make me more patriotic. Tender, loving care, pleasantries, special consultations, uncalled-for anxiety—these were the goods you had displayed before their eyes like the colourful wares of a stationery shop. Even today, I can hear you ask, in a voice full of pathos, "Nandakumar, why do you look so flushed?" The poor fellow is a simple soul. In the interests of truth, he denied having a headache, but a cold compress made of wet rags was promptly produced. I felt entranced, but still, I could sense that your excessively meek, elder-sisterly conduct had been specially requisitioned by your excessively pure nation, Bharatvarsha. A supreme example of swadeshi "didihood"—playing the elder sister in the cause of the nation.'

'Oh stop, Antu! Please stop!'

'There was an excess of falsehood within you that day, an absurd degree of pretence. You have to admit to that.'

'I admit it—admit it a hundred times over! It was you who utterly destroyed all that. So why must you rake up those things today, so cruelly?'

'Let me share the regret that impels me to say those things. The other day, you were begging my forgiveness for diverting me from my means of livelihood. I have indeed been diverted from the true path of life, yet what I could have claimed in return as recompense for that disaster has not materialized. I have broken away from my nature, but blinded by convention, you were unable to break your vow—a vow that had no truth in it. Was it not necessary to apologize for that? I know you are wondering how things came to such a pass.'

'Yes, Antu. I can't stop wondering. I don't know what power I possessed within me.'

'How would you know? The strength you women possess within you does not belong to you; it comes from the supreme goddess, Mahamaya. What extraordinary music in your voice! Creating a nebula of resonance in my mind's boundless sky. And this hand of yours—these fingers—

their touch can turn everything, true and false, into gold. Overpowered by some unknown enchantment even while condemning it, I have accepted the dishonour of a fallen existence. I've read in history books about such dangers, but I could never have imagined that such a thing could happen to someone like me, so full of intellectual pride. Now the time has come to tear apart the web of illusion. So I shall tell you the truth, however brutal it might be.'

'Tell me, tell me! Say whatever you have to say! Don't take pity on me. I am heartless, lifeless, stupid—I never had the power to convince you. That which was peerless came my way, reaching out to me. Unworthy woman that I am, I didn't pay any heed or understand its value. A treasure that comes only to the most fortunate was lost forever. If there is any punishment greater than that, mete it out to me.'

'Let it be, let it be. Forget all this talk of punishment. Indeed, you shall have my forgiveness. That limitless mercy—the mercy of death. That is what I have come for today.'

'For that?'

'Yes, for that alone.'

'Better if you hadn't let me know I was forgiven. But why did you come like this, stepping into this ring of fire? I know—I know you have no desire to live. If that is so, please give me just a few days. Give me the final right to offer my service. I fall at your feet to beseech you.'

'What use can that service be? To pour nectar into the punctured vessel of my life! You don't know how intolerable is my bitternes. What can your ministrations do for the man who has lost his own truth?'

'You have not lost your truth, Antu! Truth remains in your soul, undiminished.'

'It is lost, it is lost!'

'Don't say—don't say such things!'

'If you only knew what I really am, you'd shudder from head to toe.'

'Antu, you exaggerate this self-blame in your imagination. What you have done without any selfish desire can never tarnish your nature or bring dishonour upon it.'

'I have killed my own nature, committed the most sinful of all murders. I failed to destroy any evil from the root, destroying only my own self. On account of that sin, even if you are within my reach, we can't be united. To marry you; to take this hand of yours in mine! Why talk of such things? All black stains will be erased by the black waters of death, the death god Yama's daughter. I have arrived at that river's shore. Today, let's talk of all sorts of frivolous matters, in a lighthearted vein. Let me finish my account of that birthday celebration. What do you say, Eli?'

'I can't concentrate, Antu.'

'Anything worth concentrating on in our lives can be found only in a few light-hearted days of that kind. It's the forgettable, heavy, heavy days that are so numerous.'

'Achchha. Fine. Go on then, Antu.'

'The birthday feast ended. On a sudden whim, Nirad decided to recite the poem about the Battle of Plassey.

Rising to his feet, he struck a pose and, with dramatic flourishes, declaimed, in the style of Girish Ghosh:

Why do you depart? O you thousand sun-rays, turn back to look,
O jewel of the day, O sun! Turn back just once to look!

Nirad is a good fellow. Very simple, but he has a ruthless memory. When I had grown desperate to end the celebrations, they requested Bhabesh to sing. Bhabesh replied that without a harmonium to accompany him, he couldn't open his mouth to sing. In your room, that sinful object was not available, so that moment of danger passed. I was hoping that would bring the evening celebrations to an end, when Satu started a random argument about whether a man's birthday should be calculated by the English calendar or the sacred lunar one. Despite all my pleas, he refused to stop. The argument acquired the sharp flavour of nationalist pride. Voices rose. We were on the brink of a broken friendship. I felt very angry with you. You had made my birthday a minor pretext for the greater purpose of getting your fellow workers to assemble.'

'Don't try to tell pretext from true purpose by looking at things from the outside, Antu. I deserve punishment, but not unjust punishment. Don't you remember? It was on the occasion of your birthday that Atindrababu accepted the name "Antu" when he heard me utter it? That is no small matter, after all. Tell me the history of that name, Antu. I want to listen.'

'Listen then, my beloved. I was four or five years old at the time, tiny in stature, still lisping, with the gaze of an imbecile, I'm told. Jyathamoshai—my father's elder brother—returned from the western parts and saw me for the first time. Taking me in his lap, he asked, "Who has given this little child sage Balkhilya the name Atindra, the Great One? That is hyperbole. Name him Anatindranath, the Not-so-great-one, instead." That word "Anati", affectionately abbreviated, has become "Antu". Even to you, "Ati"—the Great One—had once appeared "Anati", not-so-great, losing his honour on purpose . . .'

Atin broke off with a start. 'I think I hear footsteps,' he said.

'Akhil!' called Ela.

'Didimoni!' came the reply.

'What is it?' Ela asked, opening the door to the terrace.

'Food,' Akhil answered.

There were no cooking arrangements in that house. Instead, from a nearby local restaurant, Akhil delivered meals ordered from a fixed menu.

'Come, Antu, let's eat,' said Ela.

'Don't talk of food. Humans take very long to starve to death. Or else Bharatvarsha, this nation, would not have lasted long. Bhai Akhil, don't feel so aggrieved with me anymore. You can have my share of the food. And then, make a quick escape—run as fast as you can.'

Akhil departed.

They sat down on the floor, the two of them.

'The birthday celebrations continued in a monotonous fashion that day,' Atin resumed. 'Nobody spoke of leaving. I kept glancing at my watch, a signal that people who suffer from night blindness would recognize. Finally, I said to you, "You should retire early, having just recovered from influenza." "What's the time?" they asked. "Ten-thirty," I answered. There were some signs of the party breaking up—a couple of yawns, people stretching themselves. "So why are you still here, Atinbabu?" asked Botu. "Come, let's leave together." "Where to?" I asked. Apparently we were to turn up suddenly at the slum where the sweepers lived, to put a stop to their drinking. I was aflame with fury at this. "So, you will stop their drinking, but what will you give them in its place?" I demanded. I shouldn't have grown so agitated. For upon hearing my outburst, those about to leave stopped in their tracks. And the usual argument began. "So, do you mean to say . . ." "I don't want to say anything!" I retorted sharply. Such abrasiveness also seemed inappropriate. In a heavy voice and with a sidelong glance at you, I said, "I'll take your leave." Once outside the room on the second floor, my legs seemed reluctant to carry me away from the spot. On a sudden impulse, I patted my breast pocket and exclaimed, "I seem to have forgotten my fountain pen." "I'll go fetch it," Botu offered and rushed to the terrace. I ran after him. After pretending to search for a while, Botu said with a faint smile, "Take a look—I think the pen is still in your pocket." I knew for sure that to find my fountain pen, it was my own abode that needed to be searched. "I have something special to discuss with

Ela," I was forced to say openly. "Fine, I'll wait for you, then," Botu insisted. "No need to wait. Please leave," I told him curtly. "Why do you get so angry, Atinbabu?" sneered Botu. "I'll be off.'"

Once again, the sound of footsteps could be heard. Atin started, then fell silent. Akhil appeared on the terrace.

'Someone has handed me this slip of paper for Atinbabu,' he said. 'I've kept him waiting on the street.'

Ela's heart missed a beat.

'Who is it?' she asked.

'Let the babu enter,' Atin instructed.

'No, I shan't,' Akhil retorted firmly.

'Don't worry—the babu is someone you know,' Atin assured him. 'Haven't you met him many times before?'

'No, I don't know him.'

'You know him only too well. I tell you, there is nothing to fear. I am here with you.'

'Go, Akhil,' urged Ela. 'You have no reason to be afraid.'

Akhil departed.

'Has Botu come here, then?' Ela inquired.

'No, it's not Botu.'

'Tell me who it is. I feel uneasy.'

'Let that be. Let me continue what I was saying before.'

'Antu, I just can't listen with attention.'

'Ela, let me finish my story. There's not much time left . . . You came up to the terrace. I smelt the soft fragrance of rajanigandha. You had hidden that bunch of tuberoses from everyone else, to gift it to me when we were alone. With the secret welcome of these shy blossoms began Antu's new game of life, played out in the arena of our relationship. After that, Atindranath's intellect and sobriety gradually declined, sinking into the bottomless depths of oblivion. That was the first time you had embraced me, saying, "Here is my birthday gift to you." That was when I received the first kiss. Today, I have come to claim the last kiss.'

'The babu has started banging on the door,' Akhil came and informed them. 'He has almost broken down the door. He says it's urgent.'

'Have no fear, Akhil. We'll calm him down before the door is shattered. Leave the babu unattended and run away immediately to some other destination. I am here to take care of Ela di.'

Ela drew Akhil to her bosom and kissed the top of his head.

'My dear, obedient boy, my brother—go away from here. I have some money knotted into the corner of my sari aanchal. Here—it's a blessing from your Ela di. Touch my feet and promise you will leave at once, without delay.'

'Akhil, you must follow this piece of advice,' insisted Atin. 'If anyone questions you, you will tell the truth. Tell them it was me who forcibly threw you out of this house tonight at eleven. Come, let's make this statement a reality.'

Once more, Ela drew Akhil close.

'Don't worry about me, bhai,' she said. 'Your Antu da will remain here, so there's nothing to be afraid of.'

As Atin began to propel Akhil out of the terrace, Ela cried:

'Let me come with you, Antu!'

'No! Not on any account,' ordered Atin.

Ela remained standing there, her bosom pressed against the low railing of the terrace. Sobs swelled in her throat in waves. She realized that Akhil had left her forever that night.

Atin came back.

'What happened, Antu?' Ela inquired.

'Akhil has left. I've locked the door.'

'And that man?'

'I've let him go as well. He was waiting, imagining that I was absconding from duty, whiling my time away in idle chat like the beginning of a new Arabian Nights. It is indeed another Arabian Nights— pure fiction, from start to finish—fiction that is utterly fanciful. Ela, do you feel afraid? Don't you fear me?'

'Fear you? What utter nonsense!'

'There's nothing I'm not capable of doing. I've arrived at the ultimate nadir of fallen existence. The other day, our team looted all the possessions of an orphaned widow. Manmatha was known to the old woman from her village days. He was the informer—the one who had led the gang to her place. Seeing through his disguise, the widow recognized him and cried, "Manu, baba, how could you do such a thing?" After that, they didn't let the old woman live. To meet the needs of our own loss of dharma—what we call the needs of the nation—her money was delivered to its

destination through these very hands of mine. It was with
that money I broke my fast. After all these days, I have been
truly branded a thief. I have soiled my hands with stolen
goods, enjoyed their benefits. Botu has leaked the name of
Antu the thief. Lest I escape with little or no punishment
due to lack of evidence, he has arranged to get an order
issued by the Commissioner, to ensure that instead of
being presented before an English magistrate via the police
superintendent, the case is placed under the jurisdiction of
the Bengali magistrate Jayanta Hajra. Botu knows that I am
bound to be captured tomorrow. Meanwhile, feel afraid of
me. I myself am afraid of the dark ghost of my dead soul.
Today, there is no one here to save you.'

'Why—you are there, after all.'

'Who can save you from me?'

'What does it matter if you don't save me?'

'Amongst your own group of companions, the ones
who were Ela's nationalist brothers once, the ones you
graced with a mark on the forehead in the sisterly ritual
of bhaiphonta—amongst those very same people, word has
gone around that you should not be left alive.'

'What crime have I committed, graver than theirs?'

'You have a lot of information; you know the names
and other details of many people. Under torture, all would
be revealed.'

'Never.'

'How can I say that the man who came here today
didn't come carrying that very order? How powerful such
commands are, you know very well.'

Ela started. 'Antu, are you speaking the truth? Is that true?'

'We have received a piece of information.'

'What's that?'

'In the dead of night, the police will come for you.'

'I knew for sure that the police would come for me one day.'

'How did you know?'

'I received a letter from Botu yesterday saying that the police are after me. He writes that he can still save me.'

'How?'

'He says that if I marry him, he can pay security for me and take responsibility for me when I am out on bail.'

Atin's face clouded over.

'What did you reply?' he demanded.

'On that same letter, I just wrote one word: "Fiend!" Nothing more.'

'I have information that it's Botu who will lead the police here tomorrow. As soon as he has your consent to his proposal, he will move heaven and earth to save you from the tiger in order to drag you to the crocodile's lair. He is so tender-hearted.'

Ela clasped Atin's feet.

'Kill me, Antu. Kill me with your own hands. I can't imagine a more fortunate fate than that.' Rising to her feet, she kissed Atin again and again, crying, 'Kill me, kill me now!' She tore open her clothing, exposing her breast.

Atin stood unmoving, stern as a stone statue.

'Don't worry at all, Antu,' Ela pleaded. 'I'm yours, after all. Entirely yours—yours even in death. Take me. Don't let filthy hands touch my body. This body of mine belongs to you.'

'Go and lie down immediately,' ordered Atin in a harsh voice. 'I command you—go and lie down.'

Ela clasped Atin to her bosom.

'Antu, my Antu! My king, my god! How I loved you, I could not fully reveal to you. On the strength of that love, I beseech you—kill me. Kill me!'

Atin grasped Ela forcibly by the arm and dragged her to the bedroom.

'Lie down!' he ordered. 'Lie down, now! Go to sleep.'

'I can't sleep.'

'I have the medicine to make you sleep right here with me.'

'It's not required, Antu. Take from me my last conscious moment. Is that chloroform you have with you? Throw it away. I'm not a coward. Make sure I die in your lap, in full consciousness. Our last kiss will be unending, Antu. Antu!'

In the distance, the sound of a whistle could be heard.